# below the line

by **sara chin**

**city lights**
**san francisco**

10 9 8 7 6 5 4 3 2 1

Cover design and photography by Rex Ray
Book design by Elaine Katzenberger
Typography by Harvest Graphics

Library of Congress Cataloging-in-Publication Data

Chin, Sara.
Below the line : stories / by Sara Chin.
p. cm.
ISBN 0-87286-331-X
I. Title.
PS3553.H48976B45 1997
813′.54 — dc21 97-27593
CIP

City Lights Books are available to bookstores through our primary distributor: Subterranean Company, P.O. Box 160, 265 S. 5th Street, Monroe, OR 97456. Tel.: (541)-847-5274. Toll-free orders (800)-274-7826. Fax: (541)-847-6018. Our books are also available through library jobbers and regional distributors. For personal orders and catalogs, please write to City Lights Books, 261 Columbus Avenue, San Francisco, CA 94133 or visit us at http://www.citylights.com.

CITY LIGHTS BOOKS are edited by Lawrence Ferlinghetti and Nancy J. Peters and published at the City Lights Bookstore, 261 Columbus Avenue, San Francisco, CA 94133.

## ACKNOWLEDGMENTS

I would like to thank my friends for their encouragement and support, Oliver Gilliland for his help at a critical point, and my editors, Nancy J. Peters and Elaine Katzenberger, who first saw these stories as a book.

To my parents, Rachel and Neng
To John and Lin
And Paul

# CONTENTS

# below the line

WHERE I LIVE the air is dense with morning business, jackdrills hammering, dust filling the streets. On the click of a traffic light — or two jumps before — all of Chinatown surges in one direction, then the next: schools of fish converging on the day's bargains, darting for the bus. It arrives, a great whale humping on broken springs. Whoosh, its doors open. Shut. Its engine roars away. In the fumes it leaves behind, a man sings in cockeyed English, "My girl — I wait ocean for you, I wait sea."

He stacks crates of mangoes, papayas, beans, and bokchoy. Down the sidewalk, and around the corner. Chives, basil, red peppers, he fills the four corners of the universe: "My girl!"

# IT'S POSSIBLE

ONE DAY I saw people making a movie of a man in the park. The man wore a gray suit and looked like a pigeon. He was short and neat and round in front. He held a briefcase in his left hand, and with his right he gestured to the camera and sang in the piercing voice of a lovesick girl.

When my uncle died, I thought of this man, I don't know why, perhaps because the stranger in the park fooled me, as my uncle did. I saw him, the stranger, in Chinatown and thought I knew at once what sort of man he was, a man of modest demeanor, restrained and correct. He wore thick glasses and had pudgy hands. He carried a fat briefcase, probably stuffed with columns of numbers. And he wore whatever was available, for on the day I saw him, he had on a suit that was too high in the waist, too short in the leg. Dressed like that, the stranger was a man without style, without definition. He let the film crew move him about, from one end of the park to the next. He didn't complain, but when the camera rolled, this man in gray, this pigeon, suddenly stood his ground and belted out a song. He wailed. He sobbed. He clutched his briefcase. And with his free hand, he embraced the world; he became a star, a star of the Peking opera. He sang a love song. It was rush hour, I remember. Cars rolled past the park, pigeons swooped, yet, through it all, the man never once faltered. His voice cut deep into the afternoon, loud, nasal, and distressing.

My uncle did not sing like that. As far as I knew, he did not sing at all. He was not an old-fashioned scholar who loved Peking opera and happily devoted years to learning female roles. He was a modern man, a serious man, a man schooled in Shanghai where money was king. Perhaps for this reason my uncle looked like a gangster. At least he did to me, but then, I knew him only in passing. I met him once when I passed through Taiwan, a second time when he arrived in the States, and finally a last time when he was dying. Three times in all, yet I thought I knew something about him.

The first time we met — this was some years ago — my uncle was living what he considered a period of exile in Taiwan. At the time, Taiwan was poor and third-world. It was run by an old generation who had fled there from the mainland. Many were military men like my uncle who thought only of going back to China and throwing the communists out. "How can you change anything?" my mother argued with my uncle then. "It's fate. Why don't you come here?" She urged him to join her in New York, where she was studying at the time. When he wouldn't, even after she took a second job and saved money and sent him a ticket, the distance between the two of them stretched into years. I might never have seen my uncle had a storm not driven me, unexpectedly, to Taiwan.

I remember how I arrived, the winds rising, my plane, diverted from Hong Kong, rolling side to side, holding level only long enough to touch down, then the sky closing in and, just a few hours later, a typhoon ripping through. It tossed trees in the road, smashed houses. The capital, where I landed, went dark and sank under a flood of sewer water. The storm swept through so fast it seemed no sooner did it arrive than it was gone. And the wind with it.

The sun came out then, fierce and tropical. It quickly burned the streets dry. Thick pools of water turned to sludge. Everything that had drowned — cars, motorcycles, buildings, trees, patches of grass — emerged higher and taller. Soon the whole city seemed to be levitating above the waterline, and the stink of the flood settled, like a film of sweat, on everything.

The day I met my uncle, I remember walking into a mirage of white light and bad smells. I had just entered the lobby of the hotel where I was staying. The air-conditioning had broken down. The front window had been reduced to a wall of shattered glass held together with strips of tape. Workmen swarmed everywhere. They slapped wreckage off lounge chairs, plants, the occasional hotel guest. Whatever stood in their way, they whipped with small white towels.

Out of this whirl of activity appeared a man dressed in a dark suit. He picked his way with military precision around the broken glass in the lobby, crossed a square of intense light and came toward me. I could not see his face. The sun was in my eyes, but even if I could have made him out, I wouldn't have known whether or not this man, this figure moving neatly through the wreckage of a storm, was indeed who I was supposed to meet. My uncle was a man who had kept to himself. He had never allowed his picture to be taken. "Because of the war," my mother told me. She had only one photo of my uncle, a faded graduation portrait, a miniature not much bigger than a postage stamp.

As he came closer, I could not match his face to the miniature, but I could see that he came my way with a purpose. He produced a faint smile. I walked toward him and we met in front of two lounge chairs. One had a mutilated rubber plant on it. The other supported a hotel guest who was not in much better shape than the plant.

We shook hands in front of these two witnesses and my uncle said, "You're here! At last!"

He dropped my hand and looked me over. He had rough, pitted skin. Baggy eyes. He was not the man I had expected. My mother said he was very patriotic when he was young. He had practiced calligraphy and studied engineering. He had been exemplary then, but now there was something tough and hard about him, something at odds with his soft hands and the perfect cut of his suit.

My uncle started to speak. Just then, the man in the lounge chair next to us sat up and belched. I moved away, but my uncle took personal affront. He called over two workmen and, though he had no authority to do so as far as I could tell, he gave the men an order and they obeyed immediately: they hauled the stranger out of sight.

"It's good luck!" My uncle turned back to me. "The typhoon! We should have had it sooner, so it could have brought you here earlier. Much earlier. We should not have had to wait so long to see each other."

He led me out of the hotel and put me in a large black American car. We sped off across the city. The driver drove fast and hard. He didn't go around flooded areas, but jammed the car straight through pools of mud and seemingly bottomless streets. I was afraid we would stall or sink into a deep hole, but my uncle said, "We won't go down. Lao Fong is too capable."

"Lao Fong," he spoke to the driver, "tell her how many children you have."

Lao Fong laughed. His thick neck bounced on rolls of fat.

"Tell her," my uncle said.

Lao Fong lifted both hands off the steering wheel. "Five plus two," he said. "Twins."

"Seven," my uncle told me. "Seven born here. Seven he still has to feed. Don't worry. Lao Fong won't do anything foolish. He can't afford to."

The car banged through an intersection. My uncle saw something up ahead. He didn't speak or point, but Lao Fong cut the car across a busy lane of traffic and pulled to a perfect stop in front of a street vendor. The vendor ran up and stuck pineapples through the car window. Big fragrant things with spiky tops. My uncle picked out three. "Take two home," he said to Lao Fong, and we drove on.

He asked after my mother, "Why does she live hundreds of miles from your father?"

"Because that's where she could get a job."

"Why doesn't she send me any pictures of herself?"

"Because she says she's getting too old for pictures."

"Can she get pineapples where she lives?"

"In Iowa?"

"Yes."

"I don't know, in the summer, I guess."

"And in the winter?"

"We eat apples."

"Red ones?"

"Yes. Red and yellow."

"Red and yellow — hmm, your mother liked apples, I remember. Yes. In Peiping we had the little ones. Crab-apples on a stick. She used to buy them everyday, did you know?"

Lao Fong entered a traffic circle that pulled in cars on one side and spun them out the other. A soldier stood at rigid attention in the middle. As far as I could see, there was nothing worth guarding in the vicinity, but the soldier stood on a pedestal and held the ground he could not yield. Perhaps he was marking a point in the center, just so there could be a circle in the first place, just so we could go around him, grinding gears and venting exhaust. It was hard to tell. The sun beat down. We whirled by, and all I saw was a white helmet, white gloves, and the angle of a face, then, as we broke free of the circle, a broad boulevard, a long, low building, rows of windows, porticos, and more soldiers, all standing guard in white helmets and immaculate gloves.

"The presidential palace, the legislature, the ministries. Built by the Japanese when they were here."

My uncle pointed out the sights without comment. My mother had told me he used to work for the government. "Before. Before the communists," she said. "Afterwards, I don't know. He didn't talk about what he did after. After he went to Taiwan."

Lao Fong passed a small park and turned the car down a dark, narrow lane. The walls sheltering the houses on either side were crumbling away. Everything was a dank gray except for the red gates that marked each house and the tiled roofs that had grown a coat of bright green mold. Lao Fong steered around chunks of cement the typhoon had thrown in the road and came to a stop in front of an unmarked gate.

"Don't think these are Chinese houses," my uncle said. "They're too small. The Japanese built them. That's why the termites are eating them all up now."

Lao Fong opened the car door, but before we could get out, the red gate swung open and my aunt stood there, holding a yellow umbrella. "Quick, quick," she said. "The leaves are falling off the trees."

She held the umbrella for me and we ran into the house. "It's the rain," she said. "And this terrible old house. You must tell your mother we're sorry we can't entertain you properly."

She gave me a pair of slippers and a maid brought in tea and fresh fruit. The fruit was precisely arranged on a tray, but my uncle would not let the maid serve it. He tested it first.

"Cold," he said, "Too cold." He dismissed the fruit and

had the maid take it away. When she returned, my uncle handed her the pineapple he had brought and instructed her on how he wanted it served: cut in wedges, with forks, at room temperature.

"You don't put fruit in the refrigerator, do you?" he asked me.

"Well," I said.

"You shouldn't," he shook his head. "Fruit kept in the refrigerator loses its flavor. It has no smell, and if it has no smell it has no taste. For all you know, you might be eating a cucumber instead of a melon, and that would be a waste of your money."

My aunt passed me a cup of tea.

"Do you have a boyfriend?" she asked.

"Don't do anything to the fruit," my uncle continued. "Just buy the best and serve it as it is. When it's ripe, of course. That way you'll preserve the taste, and each time you eat a pineapple or a melon it will remind you of many things —"

"Please," my aunt set a plate in front of me.

"It will make you remember how much you liked eating the pineapple or the melon before, and how much you will like eating it again. You will never forget."

My uncle raised a brow at me, "You understand?"

"Butter cookies," my aunt said. "He has too many scientific theories. Help yourself. Ever since we left the mainland, your uncle has been developing theories. He thinks he can explain why we are here and the bandits are there."

"Try these," she picked out a round cookie and a square one and put them on a plate for me.

"Do you have a boyfriend?" she asked. "We must take some pictures so you can show your mother and your boyfriend."

My aunt pulled out a photo album and introduced me to my cousins. The younger one was doing military service on an island in the Taiwan Straits. "He's very technical," my aunt said. "He sends balloons to the mainland."

"Messages of freedom," my uncle said.

"Yes, with the balloons. He sends them to the communists," my aunt showed me a young man with a shaved head. "When he's through, he's going to study with his brother —"

"This one," my uncle leaned in and tapped a face that looked like his. "He's studying rockets. In Long Island. Is Long Island famous for rockets?"

We lingered over the photos and the pineapple the maid brought in. It was as good as my uncle had promised. After the pineapple, my aunt went out and sprayed her hair and put on high heels. Then, before the day got too hot, we all climbed into the air-conditioned American car and had Lao Fong take us on a tour of the city.

Downtown, my aunt bought me a gauzy pink blouse and my uncle picked out an umbrella to match. "See all the girls here," he said, "their skin is so white. They protect themselves from the sun. You should, too."

"Do you want a Rolex?" My aunt stopped in front of a sidewalk display. "They're very reasonable. What will you buy for your boyfriend? A Seiko? Something Sony?"

She led me from store to store, shopping for things I wasn't sure I wanted. My uncle followed, indifferent to what we were doing, but all the while standing erect as if he were on military parade. He also sat the same way, I noticed, holding his back stiff from head to tail bone. I thought this was the result of some injury — maybe he had been shot up in the war — but later, when I asked my mother, she said, "Oh no, he was too smart to get shot by the Japanese. Or the communists. He never put himself in a position where he would lose."

"This way," my uncle entered a maze of shops. He led us through an arcade draped with T-shirts and jeans and frothy dresses that hit our faces as we passed. "Careful," my uncle paused and told my aunt to take me by the arm. With her steering me, we made our way around piles of straw hats and piles of shoes, past fruit stands and bubbling tanks of juice, through a buzz of toy robots, and into a freezing, bright restaurant.

"Mr. Chang!" the waiters all greeted my uncle at once, "Madam," they bobbed their heads at my aunt. A man with a big square face came smiling out from behind the cash register. "Mr. Wang," my uncle introduced me.

"Hello, hello. Please —" Mr. Wang pointed us to a table. He didn't wait for my uncle to order, but sent a boy directly to the kitchen, and by the time we had wiped our hands on hot towels and sampled little dishes of peanuts and cucumbers and jellyfish, the dumplings were ready. Steamed dumplings, boiled dumplings, dumplings with meat, dumplings without, a corn gruel, cold noodles, all the dishes my uncle said I had to try, heavy platters and thick bowls of it came swinging over our heads and onto the table.

As the food arrived my uncle grew expansive. Friendly, even. It's strange, but I don't recall ever seeing him really eat. Each time I was with my uncle, I noticed that he indulged in food, but he didn't seem to enjoy it in the usual way. He was always the connoisseur, the host, the one who served everyone else, doling out a bit of this and some of that, along with a good measure of his thoughts.

Over dumplings he said, "Mr. Wang," and pointed his chin at the man with the big face who had gone back to his cash register. "He used to have two restaurants like this. In Shanghai. One he lost to the communists, and the other? To a movie star."

"Worse than Chiang Ching," my aunt leaned into my face and spoke under the whir of the air-conditioning. "That actress had terrible teeth and she gambled away the second restaurant."

"Yes, but before that," my uncle said, "don't forget,

before that I ate well. Very well. One week in one restaurant. The next week in the other. Noodles here. Dumplings there. The shrimp and vegetable dumplings were the best. I ate a lot of them and that's how I misspent my youth. In a place like this."

He waved an arm at the restaurant. "You don't know, but this is just the way it was before. In Shanghai, the tables were here, like this. The counter over there, like that, and Mr. Wang the same, making money. Very successful. You don't know," my uncle said, "but nothing has changed. Here, everything is the same. Only new. And better."

He pointed to the plastic tables, the fluorescent lights, the tiled walls. A waiter saw his hand waving and came over, "Everything all right?"

My uncle waved him off. "Everything is just more. Today," he said. "More modern. More efficient. More hygienic."

He cleared his palate with a sip of tea and got up to talk to Mr. Wang.

"That was one of your uncle's theories," my aunt said. She scraped the last two dumplings onto my plate. "We were not so modern before, so that's why," she made a sauce of vinegar and soy, "we had difficulties," she added pepper, "before, on the mainland. Is that what you learned in school?"

She rolled the dumplings in the sauce. "Your mother writes me that you'd like to know what really happened. Here, isn't this better?" She watched me put a fat dumpling in my mouth. "It's the vinegar," she said. "That's what makes it good."

My aunt wiped her hands on a towel and turned her attention to my uncle. He was at the counter chatting with Mr. Wang. The men leaned their heads together, then separated. My aunt sucked her teeth. "Finished?" She gripped my arm and pulled me to a washroom at the back of the restaurant. There she locked the door and checked the toilet stall before putting her mouth to my ear.

"Everyone knows Mr. Wang left his wife on the mainland. For the communists. She begged to leave, but he said no. He said, 'You! You are too ugly to take out!'

My aunt stepped away. "You see. What happened." She pulled a compact out of her purse and powdered my face.

"All these things, how can you know? Your uncle was too kind. He got Mr. Wang two places on the boat from Shanghai. Of course, that man brought the movie star with him, but when her teeth fell out he left her, too."

She offered me two lipsticks, one bright red and the other a brighter red, then she led me from the washroom and, with Lao Fong at the wheel, we drove into the afternoon heat. "To the most famous place for taking pictures," my aunt promised.

They took me to a fairyland, a memorial dedicated to the dead leader of the country. A big white fortress, it seemed to float above the dust of this world. In a city built on miles of cement and the yowl of twenty-four-hour traffic, the memorial—surrounded by its landscaped park — appeared as a sudden breach between buildings. And, as the highest point in that opened space, it stood out. Even with the debris of the typhoon piled here and there, it stood out — a breath of air, a space in time, a caesura between then and now. A place to park a bit of history. As we drove closer, it grew bigger and whiter until finally its whiteness filled the car windows as we drew up to the front gate.

"Drive around," my uncle said. "So she can see."

Lao Fong rolled us past the front, down one side, up another. We cruised long, white walls.

"Beautiful," my aunt said.

Lao Fong parked and we walked through the gate. Once inside, I saw what my aunt was talking about, the grand monument that everyone came to see. A building that was supposed to be what it was not — something ancient and imperial — rose up at the convergence of all paths in the park. Covered with stone white as bath tiles, washed by the recent rain, it was fresh and clean beyond reproach.

My uncle led us inside. We saw exhibits, pictures of the dead leader fighting the communists, pictures of his family, scrolls, flags, brave words, retake the mainland, eternal memories, fight to retake the mainland. We went from room to room, and everywhere there was the rustle of people circling a big empty space.

"You're lucky," my aunt said, "Because of the storm, only the tourists have come out. Usually we have so many visitors here, you cannot even get through."

She explained the exhibits to me and pointed things out. My uncle preferred examining the people who came by: a young couple holding hands, only to separate when they saw him, a nanny who hauled a little boy out of his way.

"Why do you want to go see him," my mother had once tried to discourage me. "You will just ask too many questions, and he will think you're rude. In the end he won't tell you anything, anyway."

Over the years my mother had already told me what she considered the truly important things. "Your uncle graduated first in his class. When the Japanese bombed, he joined the army. Then, during the war, he met Americans, lots of Americans, so many writers, officials, Air Force pilots — he made friends with all of them. He wasn't stupid, he got a good position. Very good. You don't know," she always concluded, "if the communists hadn't come, you just don't know —"

My uncle walked through the memorial without any comment. At the end of our tour he took the lens cap off his camera and stepped outside. He led us around a garden of clipped trees and cement paths. My aunt found a bush she liked, one that had survived the storm intact, and she posed me in front of it. Then we went on to a tree, a hedge, a stone bench. We followed the path around the memorial. It was hard to take pictures against the immense whiteness of the building, but my uncle tried, and now I have photos from that day of two charred figures — my aunt and me — standing on an expanse of white steps, or one charred figure — me — smiling into the sun. Lao Fong, who knew my mother from childhood days, is in a few of the shots, but my uncle is not there anywhere. He refused to be pinned down by the camera.

When I left Taiwan the next day, my uncle gave me an orchid to smuggle to my mother. "This one has a fragrance," he said, "she will remember."

As it turned out, I forgot to take the orchid off the plane when I got home, but I remember how my uncle packed it for me. He wore a thin shirt that day. I could see his singlet showing underneath. His hair was dark and shiny, combed back off his face. People waiting to get on the plane pushed against us, but my uncle stood his ground. He put on his glasses as he always did, carefully hooking one ear, then the other; he waited for them to settle at their optimum point, halfway down his nose, then he reached deep into a shopping bag and hid the orchid safely away.

I didn't know what to make of him then, or later. I left that first visit thinking: how elusive he is. He lives in a run-down house, yet he has the use of a big American car. He's just a school teacher, yet he orders people around as if he's still in the army. He's full of contradictions, my uncle. He raises orchids, but he also cultivates the friendship of someone like Mr. Wang, who is no better than a gangster.

At the airport I waved goodbye and walked away. The plane rose. The sea tilted away. Everywhere, it was a deep, wide blue that day.

Some eight years passed before I saw my uncle again.

By then, he and my aunt had settled in California to be near their sons. When I caught up with them, they had just moved to a condo so new that the ones across the street from theirs were still empty.

The move had changed my uncle. He looked younger. He had lost the pallor that came from avoiding the sun in Taiwan, and now he was tan and fit. He was casual. He wore shorts and he'd let his hair go gray. When I saw him again, he looked and acted as if he had truly found his natural self in a place that promoted ideas like this.

"Do you know about grass?" he asked when I arrived for my visit.

He took me to his back yard, a patio that gave onto a lawn about the size of a double bed. The lawn, tiny as it was, had patches of good green grass and patches of dry withered grass.

"How can you make it smooth?" my uncle asked. He showed me the stiff garden hose he had just bought with its sprinkler attachment. "If I try this —" he bent down.

"Watch out," my aunt called from the kitchen.

A spray of water shot up. My uncle stood. I dodged into the house and closed the glass doors to the patio.

"What's wrong?" my uncle turned toward me, the water splattering against the glass. "This is very good."

He put on his glasses and held the sprinkler at arm's length. Squinting, serious, he fiddled with the settings. A gentle rain, a dribble, and then a sudden hard shower struck him in the face, but he didn't mind. He let the water drip off his glasses and soak his shirt. "Eh," he shouted at me, "I swim everyday, did you know!"

Less than a year later, he lay immobile in a hospital bed, breathing through an oxygen mask. I went to visit him, and my cousin said, "This is terrible that you have to come so far. How is your mother?"

"Not so good," I apologized for my mother. She had lost control of her car going over a patch of ice and landed in the hospital only days before my uncle was felled by his illness. In the weeks leading up to her accident, my mother had been in one of her periods of winter gloom. When the news of my uncle came, bad as it was, it somehow relieved her of her premonitions. It gave her an explanation. She said, "See, nothing happens by itself," and sent me to my uncle's bedside.

At the hospital, my cousin said, "They can't operate. They're draining fluid from his lungs. Three liters, just from the right one."

"Papa," he moved me closer to the bed so his father could see me. The room was dark, but my cousin had positioned me by the window. I could feel the sun glancing off the side of my face. I couldn't tell what my uncle saw. He sucked on his oxygen, and after a while he moved a hand in my direction. My cousin led me away, and within the week my uncle was dead.

At his funeral, many people arrived. I was surprised. I didn't realize my uncle had so many friends here. I thought he had left them all behind, some in Taiwan and, before that, on the mainland. But when he died, I saw he had built a whole new life in this country with people like himself. The funeral chapel filled with elderly men and women. Some had lapsed into a fuzzy old age, but many looked fit and distinguished. Contemporary, even, in their black clothes and slicked-back hair.

A Cantonese voice, a northern accent, some twisted dialects in between, my uncle's friends greeted each other and filled the pews. They sang hymns. They listened to the minister talk about resurrection and rebirth, the physical life taken away, the spiritual life given to us forever, amen. People coughed. The minister introduced my uncle's family, my cousins with their two PhDs, their wives, their children. They all lined up next to the coffin, and then a stocky woman brought my aunt out from a side chapel. She was crying, loud dry cries. "Whoo,

whoo, whoo," my aunt rushed to the open coffin and tried to climb in. The stocky woman grabbed her and took her away, but we still heard her cries, and before we left for the cemetery she tried to jump in one more time as the coffin was being closed.

A streak of gray sky and a light rain pointed the way to a park of perfectly groomed hills. In the distance, there was a big white radar dish, and along the road, Vietnamese graves. So many. We stopped at a freshly dug site and my aunt ran out and threw herself on the ground. She knocked her head on the wet grass. Three times before the stocky woman and another friend could lift her to her feet. "There's no need, no need," they said. My aunt pulled her arms away and then she opened her eyes, as if for the first time. Red, crusted eyes. She opened them and saw me.

"You're here!" she spoke as if she hadn't seen me before. "I told him we shouldn't go back home. I said they have their life and we have ours. Everything is too different now. What's the point, don't go, I said, but he said, 'I have an American passport, why should I be afraid?' " My aunt's voice grew shrill, "He said —"

"Come, come." Her friends tried to pull her away, but she reached out and clutched my hand.

"He said, 'I must see my family again, Ming-wei, Ming-jing, Ming-sheng. Everyone,' he said. But when we got there, when we got home, who could know, they were all gone, all of them. Everyone!" My aunt screamed at me, "Everyone!"

Her sons descended on her and led her away.

Later, I told my mother everything. As she lay in her hospital bed with her leg elevated, she said, "You have no idea, do you, what really happened."

My uncle had returned to their village only months before. He went at a time when no one at home had anything, or any way to get anything. The government had not yet told people to get rich. So, they remained poor. "In the stone age," my mother said, "poor and ignorant."

As the first son of his village to return, my uncle brought what people didn't have then: two TVs, two VCRs, four tapedecks, three cameras, a refrigerator, even a motorcycle for his brother's boy. He took so much because they had so little, and the more he spent, the better he felt. "Are the communist bandits going to come to America to give me a TV?" he said. "Or a refrigerator?"

Before he went back, my uncle made a list. A gift for this one, money for that one, a polka-dot dress for the nephew's baby, with bubbles of pink and lime. "They won't have anything so good-looking," my uncle said. He anticipated everything. He spent money like water, money his sons contributed. He spent, but he didn't waste a penny, for he was organized, careful. After some forty years away from home, he was going to go back now and show that he hadn't forgotten anyone or anything. He even prepared for how awkward it might be with some people — First Uncle's wife, for instance. She had stopped talking to him after he refused to marry her brother's daughter. He remembered and was thinking about such things just before he left; that's what he told my mother when he called her.

Yet, once he arrived home, nothing happened as he had planned. He didn't find his brother, nor his uncles, nor their wives, nor his cousins — all of the cousins had been sent away. He found only a nephew. The one who broke into a sweat when he saw the motorcycle my uncle had brought. The one who had written all the letters ferried through Hong Kong over the years, the letters saying thank you, we are happy to hear from uncle, we are all in good health, everyone, we are studying hard.

My uncle, always skeptical of things he read about the communists, never questioned these letters from home. Because he wanted to believe, my mother said, he wanted to know he could always go back one day. There, at the gate of the village he had last seen when he took his new wife to Shanghai, there he would find the past he had left behind. He would step off the boat onto the riverbank, and the severed years in between would be joined just like that, in one step. How unreasonable, my mother told him, but he wouldn't listen.

When he got home, the village welcomed my uncle with a banquet and plenty of liquor. But my uncle found something he had refused to anticipate. It was not the news that the others had died over the years and that the nephew had lied to him, taking all the money he had sent. No, this was something people in the village would never put into words, yet my uncle knew. All that was left unsaid, he knew. It was there in the way people greeted him. Their sudden silences. Their busy gestures of pouring tea and passing cigarettes and peanuts. He knew. And it was what he had feared for so long: that those who died had in some way died because of him. In the years after he fled to Taiwan, they hanged themselves, they starved, or they sickened. However it happened, they had all died in a web of consequences that led back to him, the landlord's son, the one who had joined the army of counter revolution.

"You can imagine," my mother said, "They used to call him an enemy of the people. Your uncle. A good man. A man who never squeezed the poor. A man who was honest. Too honest. Everyone in my family was too honest.

"Your uncle went home thinking he could show people who was right, who was wrong. He went back with his scientific proof — TVs are scientific proof, aren't they? — that the Chinese people can do better without the bandits. Everywhere else in the world, we are advancing. He wanted people to know this and see it for themselves. But when he got back home, he had to see, too.

"He had to see how so many had died, how no one was left, no one but the nephew, the liar. What could he say then? Who was right? Who was wrong? What did it matter anymore? They were all gone. Our first uncle, our second, their wives, our sister. They were gone. Our first brother killed himself! He jumped from the roof!"

When my uncle arrived, the village didn't want to be reminded that he had once been an enemy of the people. They saw him come with his load of presents and who knows how much money. They thought maybe he was a big shot in America. Maybe his sons were big shots, too. And maybe these big shots could do something for the village, so they gave my uncle a banquet.

"You don't know," my mother told me, "but these affairs can be most unsanitary. Your uncle said they held his banquet on the second floor of a building that wasn't even finished. Why? Who knows. Maybe they wanted to show off their big plans for the village, but for your uncle, it was the worst thing that could have happened."

*In a building with unfinished walls, in a room with no ceiling, just slabs of rough, flaking cement with a string of bare bulbs nailed up overhead to make things festive, my uncle, the party secretary, the old men at his table, and the young men at the other tables, all sit under a cloud of cigarette smoke, rising, commingling with cement dust, falling. Between the cold appetizers and the first hot dish, the wind enters the wall-less walls and pushes the evening damp into their faces.*

*My uncle sneezes. "Ganbei," the Party secretary holds up his glass. My uncle raises his, clinking, smiling, he tosses the past down his throat. The kaoliang burns, a veil of rain sweeps in from the west.*

*The nephew laughs. His friends pester him for a ride on the new motorcycle. My uncle's neck jumps from the cold, the wind cuts into his back. He thinks of all the gifts he has brought — the shiny appliances, the truckful of treasures — how could he have known, how could he not, they were, in truth, only boxes and boxes for the dead?*

*My uncle goes back through the rain to the guest house where he's staying. He sweats through the night and into the next day. Chills and fever; he coughs and coughs. He can't shake the weight of the boxes that fill his room. He flies back to his sun-drenched condo, my aunt holding his arm. The cough comes with him. Like the boxes for the dead, it fills him with reproach, it doubles him up and takes over his lungs, his heart; he coughs until he goes back to the beginning of time and there is nothing left to remember.*

"Before the fish and meat, that's when it happened," my mother said. "The cancer. It started with the banquet, I'm sure."

My uncle never smoked in his life. He never spit, never chewed tobacco, never used snuff, never touched opium, never knew the least thing about cocaine. Crack, he thought, was what Americans had with soup. All his life, my uncle ate moderately and avoided cultivating unhealthy habits. He was a man of discipline and rectitude. He got cancer from going home, that's all, that's what my mother told me.

"In the sweet by and by," we sang in Chinese and in English at my uncle's funeral, "there's a land that is fairer than day, and by faith we can see it afar."

The minister lifted his hands. "Mr. Chang," he embraced us, embraced the moment that had brought us here. "Mr. Chang, he was a good man. He was born in 1914. He moved to Taiwan in 1949. And he retired to America in 1981. A man from Kiangsu. A kind husband. Devoted father. A Christian."

My uncle's life had these many parts to it. More than I could imagine from the little I knew of him. When he died, I tried to put together all I had seen, but it wouldn't cohere. I didn't know whether I had the wrong parts or whether the parts were all there, only they were not meant to go together; they were separate, each period of his life standing on its own. Singular as milestones along a road.

During the war — was it against the Japanese or the communists? — my mother said my uncle worked hard to save the country. In the darkest days, he gathered up the gold. Trucks and trucks of it. Was it for his country or for his superiors? I don't know.

Over the years, many things I learned about my uncle seemed to come from a movieland of possibilities. What had happened and what had not were one and the same, and if in the end I could not know what was really real, I decided to remember this: whatever my uncle had done, whoever he was, as my mother always told me, "He did what he believed and he did it well. Your uncle was talented. Your uncle was most capable. Your uncle was very, very."

IN ATTITUDES OF PRAYER and supplication, a host of the faithful gather year round in the park by St. Peter and Paul's. Mornings, they come and arrange themselves in gray and untidy rows across the mowed green. In winter, when there's no rain, they follow the path of the sun to the center of the square, crows landing in black ranks behind them. They move slowly, advancing through the park as the days lengthen. By spring, then summer, they've crossed the solstice and traveled all the way to the northeast corner, to the damp shade of the cypress trees. Here, they settle in formation or drift off to a favorite spot facing the church, a band of mothers and grannies and old men. They plant their feet, breathe as one, unhinge, left, right. They lift their faces to the sky, raise their arms, and looking beyond church and steeple and flapping pigeons, they project their gaze higher still, to what must be the good father above. Seeing them, some might think they have prayer in their hearts but they're here for pagan purpose: they come to unlock joints, move their chi.

The clock in the church tower advances. The faithful stop circulating breath and limb. They regroup, the sun wrapping them in the gold perfection of first light. Never has the grass been so green, the crows so fearless. They breathe as one, the faithful, slap their faces, slapslapSLAP. They slap the day to gold, to red, to vermilion.

After a year, the best of the faithful wear sweat suits of bright yellow.

# RED WALL

*In Beijing, people are getting rich and riding around in chauffeured air-conditioning. Not so long ago, things appeared to be otherwise. I set down what I saw then. But was my experience an encounter with history, or with nostalgia? Is this just the sort of thing an American would mix up?*

THE LONG WALL never quits. It goes on, one street to the next, Zhongnanhai to Tiananmen. Lovers come, sit in its shade and, like the wall, they too go on and on, rapt in themselves, bicycles left by a tree, the traffic beyond flaring white.

Through the afternoon, people gather to buy an ice, cross the street. Buses come, veer away, yet nothing disturbs the long wall and its red shade. A march of leafy trees shelters it from the street.

I sit and watch a young soldier feed a popsicle to his girl. It's a treat to hide in the shade and eat an ice. The girl and her popsicle melt. The day's heat can only make them expire faster. The ice drips, the girl giggles over the smear on her lip. Her soldier takes out his handkerchief and applies it to her giggle.

Soon, an elderly couple approaches, two old Beijing men walking arm in arm. One swings a bag, the other leads with his belly. They pass the young lovers and come at me, hefty old men with shorts hauled up to their armpits, hair buzzed to their skulls. They cross in front of where I sit, big busy voices bowling along. They don't see they're going to trip over me until I pull back my feet. Even then they go on without a glance until a bump in the sidewalk, a crack in a thought, stops them suddenly. They turn to stare.

The lovers separate then. The girl, so flirty a moment ago, turns into a pudding face, the boy shrinks to a mere noodle. His uniform rumples, his handkerchief goes back to its pocket.

Boy and girl think the old men are looking at them, but I know they're not. The old men are staring at me. In the days before the city is entirely given over to the new, they have this look for the stranger in their midst. It's a stare that commits the whole body to its task, head up, chin out. The eyes do the calculating. They can tell whether the person stared at — like the donkey one might buy — has a set of teeth on her and enough meat to last a winter or two. This stare I recognize. I've prepared for it by wearing sunglasses. Large, expensive globes tinted to shield out UV and other rays. I've been to Beijing before. I know what to do: I smile. The old men stare. I smile again. Show a bit of teeth. They'll go now, I think, they've seen enough. But no. The old men suddenly rush me. Run me down like a barnyard chicken.

"Xiao Hung, Xiao Hung!" they shout, "What are *you* doing here!"

I jump. And behind me someone cries. Only then do I

understand: it's the girl with the young soldier. The old men really have been staring at her, not me. She runs now, Xiao Hung, her flimsy dress streaking along the red wall, her soldier following. So much has changed since I was here before.

Before, I came to work. Before, I came to meet history, to shake its hand, look it in the eye. Hang a microphone over it, record it. Before, I didn't have time to come to the red wall and rest in its shade, stare at people as much as they stared at me.

A lifetime ago it seems, Jill called one day and startled me. She said, "Would you like to do something different?"

I didn't know what she meant, but soon enough she was talking me into my first trip to China. I wanted to go, there was no doubt about that. I had relatives everywhere and I wanted to see the great sights, but even so, Jill had to convince me; she wasn't offering an easy trip. She said, "The money's not quite in place yet, all of it, but it will be, you know. This is just too fantastic to pass up. They're all dying off! We've got to interview them now or we won't get them at all, at their age. Can you do it?".

She wanted me to work six weeks for nothing, filming on a bare-bones budget, pay deferred. The days would be long, with no overtime, but naps were guaranteed.

"Absolutely. They're all incapacitated after lunch, I don't know whether it's the lunch or the heat, though having eaten some of the lunches —"

Jill planned to travel all over: Shanghai, Beijing, a village here and there. "You'll get to see a lot, though it might be awful, too, some of it." She took pains to warn me as well as win me over. Jill was an old friend. She had given me my start, hiring me for a documentary series she had produced several years earlier.

"What do you mean?" I said. I had grown up in New Jersey, Jill in London; Jill had a different idea of awful than I did. Among other things, she liked marmite and fish and chips.

"You'll see," she said.

Before I left, Jill briefed me on what she wanted from China, "A simple story."

"Good," I was relieved. "It's not going to be another thriller then."

I remembered an exposé Jill had done on British intelligence. Something about fair trade, or was it "the" fair trade? Sex for secrets, where the sex had become worth a lot more than the secrets. Jill had left London for New York after the fallout from that show. That was also when she changed her name from Gillian to Jill. "More to the point, don't you think," she said.

"No, no," she assured me now, "I'm not going to go to China and make people drop their drawers — if that's what you're asking."

"You promise."

"Please. This one's not about smutty people. This one's history."

"From those who lived it."

"Exactly. That's the point. We're going to be educational."

Jill said this last without embarrassment. She was the only person I knew who could, and did, go on TV to say, "The purpose of film is to raise the general level." She said this on public TV, but even so . . .

Jill was tall, close to six feet, and liked to cultivate the attention she always got for her height and her looks. When she talked, people had a way of stepping back, inadvertently, to get a good view of her.

She sent me her script: "China Reborn." She was going to cover forty years of revolution up to the moment of what the communists called liberation, but what Jill decided to call birth. The birth, in 1949, of the new China, long and fraught, but made momentous the instant Chairman Mao stood atop the red wall and waved those famous hands.

"I've got loads of footage already," Jill said, "Newsreels, Shanghai melodramas — you name it, it's incredible."

Along with her script, Jill included a list of things she wanted me to know about China. Her list went like this:

> *General Li:* Can we drug him? Antihistamine, of course. Otherwise, he'll come across as a crybaby. Age: 78.
>
> *Liu Bai and Liu Bing:* Brothers. Fought the Japanese. Bai is a good talker, Bing is not. But Bai can't walk (knees shot to hell). Bing can. So — who to interview? I need a tour of their village. Someone who can walk and talk at the same time. Is this too much to ask? Age: Pickled.
>
> *Chen Xiao Lan:* "Little Songbird of the Party" Will she sing for us? Age: Not apropos.

I packed for my trip: sound recorder, tape, batteries, microphones, cables, headphones. I took five cases. Then my mother called and I took six. The sixth was filled with clothes and gifts for relatives in China.

Before I left, my mother also sent me a briefing paper. Hers went like this:

> *Jiou-jiou,* your uncle. My first brother. Don't be like his wife. Don't talk so loud.
>
> *Jiou-gunggung,* your great-uncle. My mother's brother. Very old. Yell at him. His ears are no good, but he can eat. Everything.
>
> *Jiou po-po,* your great-uncle's wife. She eats everything, too.
>
> *Gugu,* your auntie. Your father's sister. If you are so short of time like you say, don't bother

with her. If she sees you, you will not get away. Believe me.

*San Jiou-jiou,* your third uncle. Also my brother. But this one is younger than the other. This one is number three out of four. Like I am number one out of three. For girls. All my family, not your father's. ( Your father's side, you call him Shu-shu, okay?) This one, San Jiou-jiou, I have something special for.

I put these notes away in my bag and went off to China. Thoughts of the film, can Jill make it work; of my family, who should I see; and of the revolution, what will it tell me, going round in my head.

The first leg of my trip took me to Hong Kong. I slept most of the way, but woke as the plane dropped out of the clouds and the harbor appeared below, an expanse of global shipping, a skyline of dominant buildings. I thought of the memorable words from an otherwise unmemorable movie: "Thank you," the beautiful Chinese mistress said, "Thank you, Taipan. Thank you."

The plane whined. Skimmed rooftops, laundry, then — whump — it set me down.

Jill was already there. She'd gone on ahead to consult with Peter, our cameraman. Peter was a big guy, Cantonese, who said whatever he liked. His favorite game was insulting Jill. He called Jill "Missy." She called him "Boy." They knew each other from their early days in London, when both had been scrounging for film jobs. While Jill went on to become an inappropriate person at the BBC, alienating one executive after another, Peter found his niche shooting documentaries in London. He was able to do this for a number of years until his mother finally faked a heart attack and forced him home to Hong Kong to run the family business.

"Shirts," he said when I met him.

"Really?" I felt a bit confused, jet-lagged, probably. Jill had told me Peter owned a factory, but I couldn't recall how she had said making shirts and making films went together. Peter, on first meeting, didn't offer me a clue. He wasn't your stereotypical Hong Kong businessman. He didn't dress his hair, he didn't wear nice clothes, he wasn't pale, or neat. He was a slob. Big olive face set off by a frizz of hair, brown, kind of kinky. Maybe he had some Portuguese blood; he said his family came from Macao. When he walked, his pants slid off his hips. He had no waist.

I asked him, "You still making shirts? Is that what you do, mostly?"

"She didn't tell you?" Peter jerked a thumb at Jill. "I make my wife do it."

"Oh, it's not like that," Jill said, "She loves it. Making money."

"Of course. That's why she's my wife," Peter laughed a high-pitched laugh.

Later, Jill said, "That's Peter. When he came home, he kept shooting film, but his family said, is that all you learned in London? Coolie work? They told him, you run the factory. But he said, no, you find me a wife. Isn't that brilliant?"

Jill had us doing our first interview in Hong Kong. It was with an ancient couple who had worked for the YMCA, running leadership programs for Chinese youth. The Chinese half of the couple was a man from San Francisco Chinatown, and his companion — I calculated they'd been together since the 1960s — was from southern California, from pioneer stock he described as strict and Presbyterian.

They were Johnny and Earl. They looked like owls, short and round. Both stood on the backs of their heels and tilted their heads up to greet us when we arrived. At first, we couldn't tell them apart, not in the dim confines of their hall, but when they led us to the front of their apartment, where the light diffused from the harbor and sky outside gave everything within a pearly luminance, we could see Earl had the speckled head and Johnny the tufts of white. Though Peter said later, and he had the benefit of seeing them close-up through his camera, they really looked the same, their eyes were indistinguishably old and baggy.

"My father had the ranch and his the grocery," Earl pointed to Johnny.

"Bank," Johnny said. "The bank was the real business."

"Can you look here?" Peter held up a fist next to his camera. He was setting up for Earl's interview. Earl and Johnny had both gone to China when they were in their twenties. This would have been soon after the First War.

I hung a microphone over Earl. If he was any good, he was going to belong to the part of the film that dealt with Western influence in China. I put on my headphones.

"He's not sitting too low, is he?" Jill stuck a cushion behind Earl. We started filming. Earl talked about going to college and finding his calling there with the YMCA.

"Why the Y?" he said. He had a big voice and used it with vigor, as if to prove to us what he had been in his youth, a man who never saw a mountain he didn't want to climb. One wall of the apartment was covered with pictures demonstrating this: there was Earl in the Sierras, Earl in the Alps, Earl in Tibet. Earl with a leg up on every mountain he ever trod. "He got around, didn't he," Johnny said.

I turned Earl down on my tape recorder.

"Why the Y?" he said in more moderate tones, "Well, it was the greatest thing. In those days, it was like the Peace Corps. We got the best men, the best ideas and we put them together."

Earl slapped his hands into a sandwich. He spiked my recording.

"They were so hungry," he spoke of his Chinese students, "Anything we could get from home. Science books, magazines, why, they just snapped them up."

He grabbed a chunk of air. Jill, who sat facing him nodded, then smiled. She did this for every word Earl said, her smile the equivalent of a pat on the head, had Earl been a dog.

He lowered his head now and looked her in the eye, "They wanted change, those students, you bet. Change, which is progress, you know, no progress without change. You want something, you go get it. That's change. That's what I taught my students. And it's still the same today — some things don't change."

He sat up. Was this a digression coming on? I looked to Jill. She held up her hand. I looked to Peter, he stayed bent over his camera, but his leg moved to where Jill could poke him if she had to.

"Young people," Earl sounded a new and belligerent note, "young people — for them, change just comes natural. They don't want to sit still. And why should they?"

Jill dropped her hand. Peter stopped. I turned off. And Earl? He jabbed a finger in our collective eye. "Look," he said, "look at the students. The kids. That's who you should be filming today. Not us."

Earl was far more interested in the present than the past. "I hate old people who talk about the past," he told us at the end of his interview, "But — sometimes you have to. You're young, you people, and what you don't know, you need someone to tell you. I'm glad to do it." He went around and shook our hands.

When it was Johnny's turn, he talked about how his father and other Chinatown leaders, Chinese patriots, he called them, conspired to overthrow the foreign Manchu dynasty.

"People forget, but we really played a part. A big part.

My father sang hymns. Went to a lot of meetings. And between the church, the Six Companies, which ran all the businesses in Chinatown, and the family associations, my father raised more money than anybody else for the revolutionaries. He was very big on making China strong.

"Also, he started something, and this was very popular in Chinatown, if he knew you were a supporter of Dr. Sun Yat-sen and the Chinese republic — and he would know, because he was the one collected the money — well, he gave you a discount at his store. Then later at the bank, too, you got loans easier."

As Johnny talked, it became apparent that his father's investments to make China strong — a printing business, a cascade of banks — had done very well, even if China itself had not, and we were now enjoying one of the fruits thereof: Johnny's living room. A room that drew light from all of Victoria Harbor below, a room so big and comfortable Peter said he'd just as soon move in and shoot the rest of our interviews there, if only Jill would let him.

Johnny sat with his room stretching out behind him, a tapestry on the wall, a lamp farther back. He looked solid, seated in a deep armchair, but when he spoke, his voice came out frail and whispery. I had to turn the microphone up as far as I could for him.

"My father was someone you didn't say no to. He asked you to go to a meeting, you went to a meeting. He asked you to give a banquet, you gave a banquet. He asked you to give money, you gave money. He was tough, my father. Had to be. In his day, in the old country, you got your head chopped off, just for looking around. Or, if you went to the States, you could get run out of town, maybe killed, just for showing up there. Plenty of people were."

"Now. What else," Johnny rolled his eyes for a moment, "Oh. Ham-yu. Yes, how about ham-yu? You want to hear about the ham-yu?"

"'Ham you?'" Jill asked.

I heard Peter click his camera off.

"You never heard of it?" Johnny smiled, "It's what every Cantonese mother cooks and what all the children love —"

Cut, cut, Jill flashed her hands, I kept rolling. Jill signalled again, but I looked away. Where was Johnny going with his ham-yu? I wanted to know. Tape was cheap. Tape was infinitely accommodating.

"It stinks," Johnny said, "Ground pork with salty fish, ham-yu. And that's what my mother fed Dr. Sun Yat-sen. Can you imagine? It was like giving George Washington stinky meat loaf.

"It was Father's fault. He didn't warn Mother, he just brought the Doctor home one day and that's all Mother had for supper. Ham-yu. Hahaha," Johnny started laughing, "Mother felt so cheap."

"I see," Jill said.

"No you don't," Johnny hiccuped, "Excuse me. You ask me about how we got rid of the emperor and all I can think of is this, ham-yu. Hahaha."

"Well, then, I guess we've got it," Jill stood up."Thank you."

"No, listen, listen," Johnny held up a hand, "I think it's like this — you still on?"

He looked at Peter, me.

"It was like this: my father didn't like how in San Francisco they put you down if you were Chinese. At that time, it didn't help any to hear how bad China was doing over there. The famines, the country falling apart. People killing each other. Foreigners, too. My father said, 'Makes it worse for us here.'

"That's why he decided it was time for a change. That's why he started supporting Dr. Sun. Because he was fed up. Not on ham-yu, hahaha. But because, you know, it stinks — yes, that's it — everything stinks, and that's when you get it. Your revolution. When people are fed up. With the stink. Now, does that help?"

"Yes, yes, Thank you. So much."

This time Jill jumped at Johnny and hauled him to his feet before he could say more.

"Bulls eye," Peter winked at me and started gathering up his camera gear.

Johnny and Earl first met through the YMCA in Shanghai in the 1920s. Their paths crossed and diverged several times thereafter. But with the communist victory in 1949, they both retreated to Hong Kong and there they eventually met again. "On the ferry," Earl said, "what a hoot." They'd been together ever since, served these many years by a skinny old amah who came out now and gave us tea when we were done.

"I was there, too," she yelled. "I was there."

The amah wanted to talk about how she had tricked the Japanese during the war, but Jill and Peter were too distracted to listen. They went off to film several boxes of old photos Johnny and Earl had collected during their years in China. This was a rare find, really, a cache of urban images from Shanghai, Chungking and Canton. I realized then, that that was what Jill was after, the old photos. The interviews had been merely a chance to squeeze out more; Jill was always after more, a story here, a story there. But with Johnny going off the deep end about his ham-yu, Jill had only Earl's interview she could use now, what there was of it.

"About a roll and a half," Peter said.

As often happened, another story was left behind. If it were me — and I have to admit I love the tangential, the ephemeral, the gossip column as much as the main story, maybe more — if it were me, I would have asked Johnny and Earl about love and longevity. Their apartment was filled with mementos of their religious faith and their devotion to each other — photos, poems, hands clasped in worship and love.

Before we left, Peter took a still photo of Johnny and

Earl sitting on their sofa. "Closer," Peter motioned them together.

"Like this?" Earl put an arm around Johnny and bared his teeth. We all laughed, though Johnny, who was proper, raised an eyebrow and shook off Earl's hand. If it were me, I would have asked them, how did you keep faith and friskiness alive?

After we interviewed Johnny and Earl, we flew to Canton where we met Alice, our Chinese guide. There, Jill discovered Alice had booked us into the White Swan, the best hotel in Canton at the time.

"Whatever for?" Jill said, when she saw the gleaming white lobby and, below it, a little stream flowing under a bridge, past a tea shop. "I told you we didn't need a place like this."

Jill had made two earlier trips to reconnoiter locations and subjects for her film. She had worked with Alice on those, and afterwards returned home to report, "We have the perfect little translator." Now, however, she felt she had to eat her words. She said slowly and distinctly, "Alice, you understand, we are not Hollywood."

"Oh, yes," Alice replied. She was new to the business of guiding film groups around China, but she had worked on a big foreign picture before. "I understand," she widened her eyes, "but they have no room. At the other place."

"The other place — didn't we book them? Months ago?"

"Yes," Alice nodded.

"Well?"

"Maybe."

"Maybe what?"

"Maybe they think we're coming last month. Not this." Alice turned her palms up.

Jill stared at Alice's palms. They were pale and soft. "Oh," she said. Alice probably had done all she could. It was Jill who had negated her efforts, Jill who had decided at the last minute to delay filming by a month, and now with Peter, me, and two bellboys waiting on twenty cases of luggage, she, Jill, was hardly in a position to argue about what might have fallen through the cracks.

"Give me your passports," she said and held out her hand.

The next day, Jill sent Alice to deliver a packet of Sudafed to General Li, the weeping general. The rest of us took the morning off. Swam in a warm pool. Napped. Mid-afternoon, we set out for our interview with an intelligence officer Peter nicknamed "The Assassin."

Whenever possible, Jill interviewed in English, though sometimes the English got in the way, as it did on this occasion:

Assassin: I did not kill myself.
Jill: You didn't commit suicide?
Assassin: No. I did not.
Jill: What?
Assassin: I did not kill. Myself.
Jill: No?
Assassin: No.
Jill: I see. (pause) What *did* you do?
Assassin: I was in charge. *I* did not kill.
Jill: But your unit, it was responsible for many deaths. You say so yourself. In your own book. See, "Confessions —"
Assassin: No, no. That is revolutionary situation. Many people die in the revolution. I, I cannot save them.
Jill: But you were in charge.
Assassin: Of course. I am intelligence officer.
Jill: So, if you were in charge, you could have stopped it. The deaths. You did not *have* to execute people.
Assassin: That's what I tell you! I never did!

Mr. Wu, our intelligence officer, had been the scourge of students during the 1930s and '40s, prisoner of the

State after liberation, then a volunteer to settle a frontier region, then a sanatorium patient, then a forgotten man, then, finally and most recently, author of a Hong Kong bestseller, translated into English as *White Terror: Spymaster in Shanghai.* Mr. Wu, now shriveled as a mummy, but still sucking hard on a cigarette held at attention upright between thumb and forefinger. Mr. Wu sat under Peter's lights and tried to tell Jill that there was a genuine distinction between a man in charge and a man who killed. It was a distinction that mattered, for Mr. Wu was saying, hey, I'm not a thug. And he wasn't. As Alice told me later, though she didn't use these words, Mr. Wu didn't get to the top by killing people. He was already there. Where he came from, his family had called the shots, run the show. It had been that way for generations. What did he need to kill for? With his own hands? Mr. Wu was insulted by Jill's questions.

"How can he say what he said?" I asked Alice, "Isn't he afraid of —"

"What? At his age? Nobody listens to him," Alice wrinkled her nose.

She was disappointed, not with Mr. Wu, but with us. Disappointed that Peter was fat. And married. That Jill and I were women. Alice wasn't interested in what Mr. Wu or any of the old people we interviewed had to say, though she did become quite attentive, later on, when we filmed old generals in Beijing who arrived in their shiny Mercedes sedans.

Alice was twenty-six. She wanted to meet someone attractive. She had studied English with great discipline. Learned to speak it with hardly an accent. And not unreasonably, she expected her beautiful English to deliver more to her than it did when she got us, Jill, Peter, and me. Three not-so-up-to-date people in crumpled cottons.

At the airport while we were waiting for our luggage to come through, I caught Alice biting her lip and staring at our shoes. Peter's dirty tennies. My black Nikes and Jill's high-tops. Green, a Robin Hood green. These shoes dashed about and jiggled before the customs officials. I had never thought before what they said about us. How klunky they made us look. How low-powered. Our shoes squished and bulged where our feet bulged. Alice, however, wore neat patent-leather flats with pointy toes. They squeaked when she walked. They also squeaked when she wasn't walking. A mere shift in weight seemed to be enough to set them off. I had to tell Alice later not to wear these shoes while we were filming. They added an unwelcome commentary to my recordings.

General Li, the weeping general, was not insulted by the gift of Sudafed, as I had thought he would be. He was pleased, in fact. He told Jill he'd had his condition for years, and nothing had helped it. He was glad now to try something new. He'd already taken the Sudafed as Alice had instructed, translating from the directions on the packet when she delivered it. Could Jill see a difference?

"Yes," Jill lied, "I think so."

Peter whistled through his teeth. He set his camera up and took a long, hard look at the general.

The old man did have large, bulging eyes, as if he had been startled at some point and had never recovered. Jill asked him about the most wrenching moment of his life, when he had surrendered his nationalist troops to the communists during the civil war. She said, " Can you tell us about that, the surrender?"

She had newsreel footage of the general himself, younger by almost forty years, walking across a black and white field, wind rippling his shirt and his hair, leaving his brow exposed. His eyes are black in the white of his face. Is he squinting or tearing up? It's hard to tell. The picture jumps up and down. Crackles with white specks. I wish I could hear the general crossing the field, the two armies coming face to face, both dressed in drooping gray, a gathering of dark forms against a white sky, men falling into line, coming to rest. The general steps up, yields his gun.

"What did you say then," Jill leaned into her question. I saw Peter zoom in for a close-up, I moved my microphone closer, too. Then we waited. The three of us. We waited because whatever the general would say, we had to be poised, camera rolling, sound rolling, to splice this moment to history. This was what we had come for, not the remaking of a great revolution — who would attempt that except as a major motion picture? — but this, this stalking of fugitive memory. We were here to stir up that beast, capture it on film as it streaked through the brush.

"What did you say?" Jill prodded.

"Nothing," the old man looked puzzled."Nothing. We are like —" he held his arms far apart.

Was he talking about the two armies or about himself, the distance between the old man and the young, the one with eyes gone wet under our lights, or the other, forever reenacting his own demise?

Above the old general's desk there was a picture of the young man taken many years before fate claimed him. In the picture, the young man had the eyes of a matinee idol, dark and dreamy. He would sit for almost thirty years in prison.

We did three solid interviews after General Li. A political officer, a peasant, a soldier. Then a day off to wash clothes, do some shopping. Nothing more for three days except five reels of platitudes, which got us to Shanghai. Then a string of remarkable interviews with people who represented the calvacade of idealists and opportunists, gangsters and workers, rich and destitute, those who had made Shanghai the great sinkhole of capitalism that it was in the old days.

One woman, a starlet of the 1930s, and later the

dubbed voice for many Soviet films, said her specialty, before she joined the communists, was love and squalor. "They like me to cry," she bent her shoulders and heaved heartfelt sobs.

Jill was ecstatic, "Did you get that, did you?" she said later. She planned to use this shot with footage she had from a 1930s melodrama, showing the same actress sobbing in front of a young, handsome, and keenly distressed worker. He has just brought her the news her father has been killed. "By the soldiers!" the young man says, "They're coming — quick, quick." He pulls the beautifully weeping girl through a door.

Another woman spoke of a bleak childhood spent in a textile mill. Then there was the grizzled old man who talked of the day his comrades were mowed down. "We were just walking," he said, "dongdongdongdong, then, wah," he brought his hand up suddenly and shot us all, Alice first — she was interpreting — then Jill, Peter, and, swinging his arm, me.

"Nineteen twenty-seven," he said, "and I was twenty-two." He chomped his teeth and glared at us.

When we finished with the proletariat in Shanghai we went on to the peasants in the south, to Jiangxi. Here the communists had had a base in the 1930s before they were forced out on their Long March to the Northwest. Jiangxi was poor and mountainous. But in the spring, when we got there, it was beautiful, the high fields yellow with flowering rapeseed, the paddy land rich as chocolate.

Peter wanted to stop and shoot along the way, at a market town, a ferry crossing, a mountain pass with a valley laid out in green and brown below. We were driving up to a village to interview some peasants there. Jill said there was no time to film GVs — general views — however spectacular they were.

Peter said, "Didn't you tell me you needed to show where all this was happening?"

Jill said, "No, I think I have it. On the old newsreels."

"What about transitions. Exteriors?"

"It's not that kind of film."

"You're not going to shoot anything else?" Peter's voice cracked. "Just talking heads? Talking Chinese?"

"Well, what else do I need? We *are* getting voice-overs. In English, my dear."

"Ooh luvly," Peter pitched his voice higher than usual. "That'll really make your film, Missy. Talking heads that aren't doing the talking."

At this point, I joined in. I was disturbed that most of my own efforts would end up in some netherland where original sound tracks go when they get mixed out of a show and replaced with voice-overs and uninspired music. I told Peter to quit harping about his shots. At least most of what he did would stay in the film. In fact, he was the film in a way that I couldn't be the sound.

"Tell her to use subtitles then," Peter got mad at me.

"Look, look," Jill intervened, "Didn't I tell you both? This is it. This is all I can give you: interviews, interviews, interviews. I don't have the bloody money for reconstructions. I can't give you the Long March, Peter."

"Who wants the Long March? All I'm saying is, open up your film. Get a shot of a village. Show the river they drowned in. The mountain that killed them. You know. It's what you're always talking about." Peter turned to me, "Isn't she?"

"Sure," I cribbed one of Jill's favorite lines, "Film is drama."

After this, Jill wouldn't speak to me for several days. She felt I'd betrayed her by siding with Peter. I felt I was merely asserting my rights democratically. Alice was fascinated by all this, by the way we tossed our opinions around. She would only smile when we asked her what she thought, really. We told her, if you're going to work on a film like this, where you don't make any money, at least you can have a good time and speak your mind.

Given the green light, Alice did start opening up little by little. Soon, with Peter's help —"Alice, Alice, you have a big rich boyfriend, hahhhh?" — she had even produced a picture of an L.A. camera assistant she had met on her last job, a curly headed guy she was writing to now.

"Where is West Side?" she asked. "Near Disneyland?"

"Let me see," Peter took the picture Alice had pulled out for us. He made a face, "Aiya, don't waste your stamps on him."

We were like this at the beginning of our shoot, fooling around every day, with even our driver joining in. He had many questions for Jill, passed along through Peter or Alice, who translated. Questions about Jill's height. Her age. Her eligibility. And her hair. Is it really red?

"My god," Jill said, "Can't you see?"

"Hung Xiao-jie," the driver got quite chummy, "Miss Red." He was our movie star, cigarette plugged into his mouth, big smile sliding off the side of his face. "You don't like marry?" he turned to look at Jill as he drove straight for whatever was in front of us, a tractor, a truck. He had quickly realized this was the best way to get Jill's attention.

By our third week, however, the spark of being on the road, the seduction of it, the feeling of walking into high adventure akin to walking into a new relationship, had worn off and a certain dull inevitability set in. Jill didn't have the money to put us up in clean hotels, so we stayed in third-rate places. In the cities this hadn't been too bad. We often went to the good hotels to use a bathroom, drink coffee. But once we ventured into the countryside, it seemed we got up in the mornings, ate bread, bread so white it didn't even look like bread, then boarded our van, only to drive madly, horn blaring, to the next moldy bed, the next dripping toilet.

I remember a hotel in the south. One of those Soviet-style buildings that looked like it had been designed by somebody who built dams. It had a big dirty façade. Corridors wide enough to drive a pickup truck through, walls varnished a mucky brown, carpets well-greased. And rats gnawing in my room.

The first day there, I went out to pace the corridor and consider my options. That's when Peter appeared. He was carrying his camera, on his way back to his room.

"Did we shoot today?" I was alarmed that I might have missed something.

"Relax. I just liberated a roll of film, that's all. They back yet?" Peter inquired about Jill and Alice. They had gone off early in the morning to negotiate filming fees with local officials.

"No. You get any good shots?"

He made a face, "Looks like shit out there. The lake," he started down the corridor to his room.

I followed him, "You were going for exteriors?"

"What else. Missy's going to be happy she's got them later. But I wouldn't mention it now."

Peter went into his room and put his camera away. I watched. There must have been something about the way I was watching, an edginess, a certain tension that got to him, for when he finished what he was doing, he said, "Okay, okay. Come on."

He led me to the back of the hotel, to a big empty balcony. There I saw he had already set up a little survival unit for himself: a charcoal burner complete with palm-leaf fan, battered pot, and chopsticks lifted from the hotel dining room.

"Hungry?" he set me to work with the fan. While I tended the fire, he disappeared for a few minutes, then returned with a couple of packages of instant noodles, scallions, two eggs, and two bowls.

I leaned on the balcony wall and ate the noodles that Peter cooked for me. The city was a brown soup below. Blocks of red brick buildings. Dusty trees. I glared at all this, the ugliness down there and its unchecked sprawl into the distance, where, smack on the horizon, there rose a smokestack that failed to belch.

"You just can't see the smoke for all the smog," I said, "I bet you it's there, though."

"Probably," Peter shrugged.

"Did you see the dining room downstairs? The tablecloths?"

"Grease on grease."

"Yeah. But why?" I must have said this with some vehemence, more than I intended, for Peter stopped what he was doing then, drinking a bottle of pop, and squinted at me. "They're all standing around," I said.

"What's wrong, you want to make them work?" Peter smiled. "What do you care?"

I had become so intent on recording all the history I could on this trip, hooking straight into other lives with my microphones, and these lives coming back to me through my headphones; I'd listened so closely to the spit and gurgle of history that I had started to take everything personally. There were the good guys and the bad, the worker, the spy. There were the good deeds and the ignoble. The workers at the government guest house who wouldn't clean their tables had failed me in some way. They made me angry. Standing about picking their faces. What did I think the revolution was about? I don't know. But one thing for sure, I didn't want to touch its dirty linen.

Peter didn't like the dirt any more than I did, but he didn't care if things weren't living up to expectations. "They're going to do whatever they're going to do," he stuck his chin at the brown ether beyond our balcony. He wasn't worried about any day of reckoning, the communists could have Hong Kong. He had his own life.

"I got a house in Sydney," he said, "You come visit me, you'll feel better. We'll make a nice movie there, huh?

Lots of beautiful scenery, Academy Award shots. And when we're done, I'll take you to Bondi Beach. You want to go to Bondi Beach?"

We left the city to go deep into the mountains. There, we interviewed peasants about their struggles with landlords and the armies that had swept through. Our best footage came from an old lady with the voice of a duck. We filmed her sitting on the threshing floor in front of her house, wet fields behind her and a boy on a water buffalo taking forever to cross through our shot.

"Xiao Hung, Xiao Hung," the old lady yelled at her grandson to get out of the way.

He whipped his buffalo up to where we were, got off and stood, gape-mouthed, listening to what the old lady had to say.

"They sold me," she described being handed over to right-wing troops. "Not even to a poor officer, but to a nobody. And me, I was pretty, too. Everybody said." The old lady wiped her face with the side of her hand. She was not crying; she was angry. "Sold to the cheapest fool around. Ai, he looked just like this one," she suddenly pointed an accusing finger at her grandson. The boy backed off, frightened.

"All right, all right," the old lady shouted at him. "You're a good boy." She was quite deaf.

When we returned to Shanghai, Jill heard she had received only part of the money she had counted on to complete her film. After her China shoot, she had originally planned to go on directly to Taiwan to interview the die-hard anti-communists there. Now she wasn't sure she could.

She cursed Johnny. Johnny, of Earl and Johnny in Hong Kong, had apparently promised the money she needed, some his own, some from his father's old connections, but none of it had showed up yet at Jill's bank in New York.

This news, coming after our argument about opening

up the film, put Jill in a tough spot. She dropped a village she had planned to include. She pored over her schedule with Alice, trying to cut it down. And she spent an evening in my hotel room, talking compulsively about how she could make the film work. This was the film that was going to put her back on her feet, restore her reputation as the terrific filmmaker she knew she was.

"I'm not going to babysit any more people," she said. "Let them bollix up their own films. They're getting the credit for it anyway."

"What do you think? Can we make a film about China for the average Joe? Who *is* the average Joe?"

"I dunno." I was washing my socks at the time she insisted on bringing this up.

"Come on, you're American."

"He likes people?"

"Okay."

"And he identifies," I unplugged my wash basin, "with them."

"Christ," Jill flopped on my bed. She stared at the ceiling while the wash basin sucked the water down.

"Maybe," she said. "Maybe what I need is a face." She sat up.

"Isn't that what we've been getting all along? Mrs. Lu, Mr. Yang, Mr. Wu," I listed the people we had filmed.

"No, not them. A face that tells it all. About the revolution."

"All right, all right." I thought a minute, recalled the smile and the famous mole. I squeezed out my socks. "What about Mao?"

"Jesus," Jill almost came over and hit me. "Don't you think I have any original ideas?"

I had only meant to point out that she did have some powerful images, like the footage of the celebration at the founding of the People's Republic. All the big faces of the revolution are there, standing on that famous wall overlooking Tiananmen. And Mao, the biggest face of all, waves his hand and says in that funny voice of his, "To-daay . . . the Chinese People . . . have stood up."

I thought that told it all, but Jill said it wasn't enough.

"Wonderful, wonderful, wonderful."

Two days later, I had taken temporary leave of Jill and the tensions of her film. I was in Beijing by then, sitting in my uncle's apartment. This was my third uncle, San Jiou-jiou, my mother's favorite brother, the one she had said I must see. My uncle lived alone, his wife had died and his daughter worked in an industrial city to the north, yet he had a surprisingly large place to himself. He didn't have to share with another family, as far as I could tell. My uncle's apartment was plain, but adequately furnished with a big glass-covered desk in the main room and an arrangement of stiff chairs that looked out over a dusty courtyard.

I was sitting in one of the stiff chairs, showing my uncle the books I had brought for him: *The Lady of the Lake, The Big Sleep,* a Ross Macdonald, an Elmore Leonard, a Tony Hillerman. All Americans. And then, yes, the latest Le Carré, too.

"Wonderful, wonderful," my uncle stacked the books on his desk as if he were stacking coins. Next to the books was a bottle of cognac. I had brought this, too. "Very good. Together." My uncle pointed to the cognac and the books.

He had a paunch, but his hands were slim and fine as a woman's. "For diagnosis," my mother had told me. "Doctors there, they don't depend on tests, they use their hands. Like your uncle — he's the best."

My mother was not modest when she told me about her family and what I should be living up to. She had not added, though, that this uncle also had his vices and enjoyed them thoroughly. He lit up a cigarette now and took a long drag. I'd brought him Dunhills.

"Los Angeles," he smiled at me.

"Yes," I said.

"You went to school there."

"Uh huh."

"UCLA."

"Film school, yeah. Documentaries."

"It's good?"

"Mmm, I guess so —"

"Your mother says it's the best."

"Oh. Then it must be," I smiled.

My uncle laughed. He knew my mother's ways as well as I did. I'm sure he'd been receiving letters over the years recounting in detail this or that milestone passed. My mother, the only one in her family to go to the States, felt driven to make the most of her opportunities. This had made her high-strung and nervous, while my uncle, though he had suffered through the Cultural Revolution like so many others, had fared better in a way, that's what I thought. He had an assurance that my mother lacked. He knew Beijing was his world in a way that my mother could never feel New Jersey was hers. And he demonstrated this to me that very day, when he took me to his friend's house. The friend was an old and favorite patient of his.

"You went *there*?" Jill was astounded when I told her later.

"Yeah. It surprised me, too, but going there, it was like, nothing different, you know? We drove over and they waved us through a gate and inside, I lost track, but way in, we came to this place, kind of hidden, and we stopped, and this kid came out and he said, 'Uncle Liang, Uncle Liang.'

"He was just calling my uncle that, my uncle's not his real uncle. Anyway, he ran up and my uncle said, 'This is Mee-kee — as in Mickey Mouse.'

" 'Go get your cars,' my uncle tells Mickey and they went off, the two of them. They disappeared all of a sudden and left me standing in the driveway, with the guards looking at me. They didn't say anything, so I didn't say anything. I just stood there. Lucky thing the kid came back. He had two cars now and he wanted us to race them. Remote control. He wasn't real coordinated. I got bored. I was thinking about crashing my car into one of the guards just to see what would happen, you know? But that's when my uncle showed up. And that's when I met him."

"You're kidding."

"No, it was him. I swear, the guy who took over from Mao. What do they call him, the paramount leader? He's old, right? And short, real short." I drew my neck into my shoulders. "Like his pictures, exactly. You remember how he looked visiting Jimmy Carter in the White House. Anyway, I said, 'Sir,' I didn't know what else to call him. And he says, 'Thank you, thank you.'"

"To you?" Jill was incredulous, "What for?"

"I'm telling you — because I brought him what he needed. Knee braces."

"Knee braces?"

"Yeah. Made out of spongy cloth. You know, you wrap it round your knees and the velcro keeps it in place? It's what you get from your chiropractor."

"All right, all right — so then what?"

"Then he was happy. Because I brought him the braces. His knees have been giving out on him since the Long March."

"Terrific. He was so grateful to you he patted you on the back and he said, 'Good work, old girl.' Was that it?"

"No, come on. He wanted to talk.

"With you? About what?"

"Hollywood."

"Hollywood?" Jill's voice shifted a register.

"I'm not kidding. Really. He wanted to know how far it was from UCLA to — let's see — Disney, MGM, and Steven Spielberg. Major studios. That's what he had on this piece of paper. He just went down his list: how far to here, and here, and here. By car."

"Bullshit," Jill turned away.

"No, wait, wait. You're missing the good part. The old man's got a granddaughter, Mickey's older sister. Well, this granddaughter is going to UCLA, see? That's why the old man wanted to talk to me. Because his granddaughter is putting the squeeze on him. She wants to get rid of her bodyguard and get her own car. To make movies, she says. But the old man won't give her a car. He says she'll kill herself in it. Or use it to get drugs. Isn't that something?"

I thought I had delivered a great story to Jill, but once she believed me, she got upset that I hadn't talked to the old man about our film.

"You didn't ask him for an interview?" she was appalled.

"Well, it's not like I could," I said.

"You were there."

"Yes, but he set the agenda. He wanted to know about Hollywood. 'Why do you need a Porsche to make a movie? What's wrong with a Benz?' That's what he wanted to know. Not this," I waved my hand at the pile of luggage we had waiting on the curb. We were loading our van for another day's work. "He won't give us an interview just like that," I tried to reason with Jill. "Even if he is my uncle's patient. He's getting too old. He's got other things on his mind. You have to be like a major network before —"

Jill walked off and boarded our van.

She wanted a face that told it all. I thought she had it, many faces. Big, fat, thin, and small. Over the weeks, Peter had given her a gallery of film portraits. He was truly a master of his medium. He didn't light a subject so much as he found the perfect light to bring forth his subject, putting a peasant woman by her window, bright quilts behind her; sitting a famous general in a big chair, half his face falling into shadow, the other half swimming with his thoughts, in and out of watery sunlight.

Jill had all of this already in the can. But what she wanted was something we couldn't give her. The way she saw it, the face that told it all had to be a particular face: the face of a very high Party official. It wasn't enough that we had filmed bureau chiefs and the directors of cultural institutes. Old generals who had big houses in nice compounds with guards and drivers. These were not people to be sniffed at, but in Jill's view, if they were retired or only figureheads now, they were not quite first-rank. What she wanted was someone right from the inner circle, someone who could get her through that red gate into the heart of things, into Zhongnanhai, where only the select lived.

"What about Chou En-lai's wife?" I heard her say to Alice.

Jill spent the remaining days of our shoot huddled with Alice, usually in the front of our van. If she spoke to me, it was only to give instructions. Otherwise, she didn't want to be reminded that I had met the biggest fish of all and let him go.

I spread my gear and myself across the back seat of our van. We drove through the alleys of Beijing. Gray walls. Curved roofs. I was coming face to face with my own history for the first time.

I thought: Jill had to stick to facts. That was the problem. She had to make this history credible. But not me. All I had to do was hold out my microphone and listen. Listen for the past to percolate up out of people. And it would come up, sometimes with more gas than I could accept; I used a beautifully pristine German microphone that easily picked up half-digested meals, ill-cooked thoughts. Can you say that again? I would have to interrupt to get it right, a clean recording. It was my job to stand watch over memory, roll my tape out before it like a red carpet. I didn't have to worry about facts or truth. I could ponder other things. Things closer to my heart.

Like when we went to the village north of Beijing and interviewed the Liu brothers, the one who could walk but not talk, and the other who could talk but not walk. Two old guys we put in a cart and filmed as they took us around their village. From tunnel to trench to wall, Jill had to cover the sure ground, going from fighting the Japanese to shooting the local landlord. But me, I could step away for a moment. Catch the young man riding by on his bicycle, girlfriend on the back. She turns, her face ghost-white with astonishment, she is wearing the local make-up, garish, she turns too quick to look at me and throws her young man off balance.

"Xiao Hung, Xiao Hung," he cries as their bicycle weaves crazily down a rutted lane. White-washed walls on either side.

Jill had to get the big picture, but I could indulge in the small moments. Another day, our last day of shooting, we filmed the Songbird of the Party. She sang revolutionary songs for us. We filmed her in a hard, bright room, the glass doors to her bookcase jittering as a truck went by outside. I recorded her pure soprano; she was still quite youthful — black hair, lush lips — she had been only a young girl when she married a famous Party leader. He had passed on in the prime of his life. Of illness, Alice told me, not political intrigue.

I asked to use Madame's facilities after we were through, and her guard, a raw country boy from the look of him, led me down a hall to a door where he stopped and averted his face. I opened the door and walked through. Inside, there was a realm of private indulgence I hadn't seen in a long time: flush toilet — dressed the American way in something pink and fluffy — white bath, shiny faucets. There was a vase of flowers, plastic, by the curtained window. And a bar of soap, pink Dove, in a green soap dish. The towels were fresh.

Jill had to ask the Songbird about Yenan, the famous

communist base in the Northwest, the one where many romances started and the one from which an ardent generation launched their final drive to power. Jill had to ask the Songbird about this, and then about her propaganda work. How she had spread the revolutionary message and advanced with the army as the communists swept to victory. We had come now, in the film's journey, to the end of the civil war, and Jill needed to march straight through to her conclusion. But I, I would have said, after I saw the oasis of the Songbird's bath, I would have said, "Tell me, madame, about your husband. I heard he was handsome, and apart from being a very reliable administrator, he was also a great ham and loved to write skits."

If I dared, I would have said this, for where Jill had to be high-minded, I loved the low ground, the things that people pushed offstage, the gossip, the dirt. I was looking for the heart, the trashy heart of my history. After all, wasn't that where the unknown leaped out at you?

When I returned to Beijing some years later, I went back to the red wall and sat, waiting for something, I couldn't say what. I saw a girl and a soldier flirt over a popsicle. When they ran off, I waited through the afternoon and watched the light turn rosy, then gold. Soon it dropped to an afterthought and the old men went away, the checker players, too, the clerks in their white shirts, the visitors from out of town. When all had left and the city went dark, with only the dimmest street lights remaining, I walked around the wall.

Jill had finished her film and seen it broadcast to good reviews. Then Tiananmen came. And it seemed no longer possible to remember the past, except for the blood it left behind.

The revolution we had filmed, the old people we had talked to, they seemed as remote now as if we, the filmmakers — foreigners, no less — had made them up, their stories and their faces. As if we had written the script, cast the characters ourselves: "Landlords, anybody want to be a landlord?" And then directed the whole thing, badly at that.

"Mr. Mao, Mr. Mao, can we have you say it again?"

"The same?"

"Sure, don't change a thing."

(All rise) "Today, the Chinese People Have Stood Up."

I walked through Tiananmen and around the Forbidden City. The night had drained all color away, the red of the imperial wall, the green of the trees. I moved through a grayscape. A small bridge opened to the left. I crossed a pungent moat below. The great wall in front. I turned at its base and walked down a narrow path, squeezed between the wall, which rose thick and black to my left, and a row of squatter tenements tottering at the edge of the moat.

Perhaps it was the night and the calm it induced, the feeling of people retreating into themselves, so many mashed into a tiny space along that strip of wall, every inch animated with people washing, gargling, eating a late bowl of noodles, pissing, yet all of this done as if under some kind of blackout, no one talking above a murmur, only a bicycle whirring past.

Perhaps it was this, the grayscape without hard edges, the calm before sleep, that made it possible to reclaim illicit thoughts, retrograde emotions. I walked along that wall, everything dark but for the man who came out in pale pajamas and read under a dim street light, but for the chess players in their white undershirts, everything dark but for the green smell of the squash plants, the beans, the flowers planted so densely along the base of the wall. I walked by and a nostalgia took over.

It had no meaning, really, except that for me, stranger to the motherland, walking along the edge of that ancient wall, along the memory of a great past, I wanted to be able to claim it as my own, not only to claim it, but to believe it was indeed a splendid story, a story of more than blood and avarice, a story worth passing on.

I remember I waxed as nostalgic as the moon that night. I came to one end of the wall, crossed the moat, turned, and continued down another side. There were no tenements now, but bushes and trees planted along the moat.

I walked on imagining my history until I noticed the bushes I passed seemed to be taking on a life of their own. They shook, more than necessary — there was no wind. Then I noticed bicycles parked by the bushes, and here and there, I saw a bush that had acquired a limb, usually shod, and trembling. Soon I noticed the biggest bushes had motorcycles, not bicycles, as if some Darwinian law had decreed the biggest and best bushes got the biggest and best wheels. In this case, Suzukis.

What I saw walking along the wall was nothing grand and enduring. Just couples making out. Some law of perverse logic must have said that bushes grown luxuriant with leaves by day had to give shelter by night to couples with no other place to go, couples desperate to develop a people's history and pass it on to new generations. It was weird. A just exchange. The night's maneuverings stripped away my illusions, and in their place, what did I have? A little hot romance?

Was this why I went to the red wall each time I returned to Beijing? Like a camel to its oasis, a horse to its watering hole, maybe I first sought out that wall, drank in its splendor, rested in its shade, just so I could wait for a moment like this, suddenly, to claim me.

I came to the end of the wall. A tower hung over the water, a moon over the moat. Far away, there were firecrackers. It was the seventieth year of the Communist Party. It was a night made to hunt for love and history.

WHERE THE STACKS RISE to the ceiling, where everything clamors for attention: the ranks of tin cans, blue and red, the piles of cellophaned noodles, the packets of spice, the bins of translated life forms — shrimp dried to pink whorls, scallops to nuggets, smelt to a mass of silver eyes — there, above it all, in a frame of indifference nailed to the wall, in black and white on the tiniest of monitors, people crowd into their own movie. It must be good, so many arrive; they're jamming to get in.

Blowsy heads pass into the TV screen. Wander its smudgy aisles. Return. From the front, the heads look no tidier than from the back. But they know what they have to do: they walk their bad hair up to the security camera. The screen goes black.

Now the music comes up, from somewhere behind the tinned abalone, a love song falling through the red labels, the disordered shelves. It pushes people out the door.

One movie finished, the next begins. Again, there are the smudged aisles, empty now. They invite you to recede into their fuzzy distance. Enter therein and select a jar of bean sauce. You can star in your own movie. Already, it's playing on the TV above — look, there, next to the plastic altar — it's you, your hand, and the moment you find your hoisin.

# FEVERS

MY MOTHER LOVES VIOLENCE. She is what the neighbors call the nice old Chinese lady down the street. She is kind and gentle and communes with green and flowering plants. Orchids and peonies, violets, sweet william, all the flowers of god's creation are her truest friends, but somewhere deep in the byways of her being, she loves Scarface, James Bond, and Dirty Harry. My mother is a devotee of mayhem and this story is for her.

## I

Wap, wap, wap! A man with his back to the camera beats another man in the face. Both men stagger.

"Is it on?"

"Of course. Can't you tell?"

— Wap! —

"They're not doing anything."

"What do you mean? They're slugging each other."

"Hahh? Don't sound like it. Turn it up."

"It *is* up."

"Hahh? They're not doing anything!"

"Okay, okay —"

WAP, WAP, WAP! Two men thrash across a dark room. One is skinny, the other big. They spin into a mirror — Unh! — Bright shards of glass fall.

The big man throws himself at the camera, blocks the light. His right arm comes out of the darkness and pounds into a face. The face explodes. It belongs to the skinny man. He crashes to the floor and pulls the big guy down with him. The two men bounce off a table and roll into the dark.

My mother strains to see them on her TV. She wants to know which man is where, on top or on the bottom, she can't tell. The picture before her is filled with shadows. The myopic dark makes the two men one, one darkness roiling up from the floor.

Wap! — The man on top administers the final blow. He breathes hard, doubled over from exhaustion. He holds my mother in suspense through four rasping breaths, then he turns to look at the camera. His right eye lifts, part of his mouth follows, he tries a smile.

"It's him!" my mother cries.

She sees that the man facing her is the skinny one, the one who was getting beat up at the beginning. Now he's come out on top and she likes it. She likes it when people at the bottom turn the tables on people at the top.

"What's his name?"

She points to the skinny man. He has the jaw, the shelf over his eyes and the squint, just like Dirty Harry. My mother's English isn't good. She doesn't get jokes like, "Go ahead, make my day," but she's watched Harry from the time she first saw him riding the range in his leather chaps. Ever since, whether he's played cowboy or cop, she's been faithful to him, and over the years he's rewarded her; he's given her a keen eye for young men with tight jaws, lean hips, and an attitude.

"Who is he?" she says now of the skinny man on the screen.

"It's Joe," I say, "and the guy he just beat up, the big guy, he's Tony."

Tony sinks to the floor. Joe walks away.

"Go back, go back," my mother says, "I didn't see."

"What?"

"The other one."

"What're you talking about?"

"Him, him."

I rewind the picture back to the end of the fight. Joe is getting up off the floor. For a moment, as his feet clear the frame, Tony's face rolls into full view. I click the freeze frame on the remote control, and Tony trembles before my mother's gaze. Now her eyes are fixed on a realm known only to her, a realm where the sounds of this world don't penetrate, for she has gone over to Tony's side.

And Tony, staring out at my mother staring at him, shudders in his own, video-charged aura. He looks like the sort of person who could be anything: he is young, he has a nice brown face and thick, springy hair. He could be Black, Latino, Black-Latino, Afro-Carribbean, some Chinese mix, maybe. His eyes are long, his nose wide enough, maybe he's even from the islands farther west, Hawaii, Okinawa. He has an elastic face. If he were an actor and not Tony in this story, he could play anyone, even the part of a white man, so long as the white man's part isn't just for a white man; Tony has a lot of potential in his face. He could be so many things he has my mother puzzled. "He's too mixed up," she says.

Her eyes are bright; she's speaking to a dream within herself, I know, I can see her dreams piling up like clouds of infinite Buddhas painted on a sacred scroll. Her hair is white, her shoulders thin as a child's. "How can he be the bad guy?" she says.

"Can I move on?" I have to shout to get through her veil of longing.

— Unh! — Joe plants a hand on Tony's face and pushes himself to his feet. He crosses to the far end of the room and goes behind a sofa to peer through Venetian blinds.

Outside, the street is dark. Joe checks to see if the world he knows is still in its place — the sickly trees anchored in cement, the usual cars wedged into their parking spaces. Across the street, the wall of apartment buildings remains unbroken; nothing moves. There is only the girl stretching her hamstrings in a window.

Joe turns away. His jaw hurts, he needs an antidote. He goes to a cabinet set in the wall, opens it, but it's empty. There are no bottles. He retreats to a back room, his kitchen. He pours himself a drink, then pours another. He takes this out to Tony who is now trying to sit up on the floor of the living room.

Joe grabs Tony by the collar and pours the drink down his throat. The liquid slops all over. It fizzes on Tony's face. "Shit," Tony shakes his head like a dog coming out of water. "Coke! *Diet* coke —"

Joe slaps him. He falls to the floor and hits his head.

"Jesus," Tony winces, "don't take everything so personal. If you don't have nothing to drink —"

"Shut up."

Joe hauls Tony over to the sofa and throws him down. Tony sinks into the mushy old cushions. His head snaps back, his knees come up; he looks like he has a crummy seat at the movie theater.

Joe pulls up a chair and sits across from him. He acts as if he's known Tony all his life — and he has. He's a cop. He makes it his business to get close to people like Tony. Tony, the kid who grew up on the edge of Chinatown; Tony, half-

Cantonese and half whatever else. On the street, Tony used to be called "Chief" because he was big and never talked. Then he got strung out and everyone called him "Sitting Duck." Tony, the kid who never knew when to quit.

"You look like hell," Joe studies Tony. He waits for the junkie tremors to take hold, then he says, "Who sent you?"

Tony jiggles his knee.

"Who sent you?"

Tony wipes his face, brushes his sleeve with his hand. He rubs his shirt, his thighs. Joe lets him. He isn't disgusted, he understands when a man needs to clean himself up. He waits for Tony to finish, then he leans forward and deranges Tony's face. Blapblapblap!

Tony sinks. Joe offers to pull him up. Tony swats him away. His neck catches the back of the sofa again, his knees come up, get in Joe's face.

"Who sent you?"

Joe talks over the knees. He sounds friendly now. "Speak up," he says, "she has to hear you."

"Who?" Tony looks around.

"Her," Joe points to my mother.

"Hello," my mother lifts a hand and waves, first to Tony, then Joe. "Hello," she waves and holds her smile; she doesn't know what else she's supposed to do.

"What's your name?" Joe asks her.

"Mary. Mary Wong."

"Mrs.Wong. Ma'am." Joe reveals he can be a gentleman; he smiles at my mother now. "I went to police academy with Harry," he says. "Harry's told me all about you. We go way back, Harry and me. Harry used to use Tony as his snitch, then he turned him over to me. Wish he never had."

My mother purses her lips. I think she's going to say, "Baloney." That's one of the first English words she learned. For years she fed babies, changed diapers, and dumped bedpans. She learned to say baloney then and I think she'd like to say it now, but she sticks out her lips and reaches for her cup of tea instead.

Joe turns back to Tony. "You hear that? Mrs. Wong is Harry's friend. Harry's seen her at all his pictures, so come on, don't waste her time. Tell her, who sent you?"

Joe throws a jab at Tony. Tony puts his hands up, "Goddammit."

He turns and looks straight into the camera, through layers of zooming lenses, he looks until his eyes get so big my mother falls into their deep, dark depths.

"I don't know what he's talking about," Tony tells my mother. He points to Joe. "And he don't neither —"

"Heyheyhey," Joe interrupts, he's not going to let Tony get off the hook by griping to my mother. He wants to get Tony pissed now, and he knows how to do it. After all, Tony's a guy with a police report that says, "Suspect reads with his finger."

"Tony," Joe says, "Do I have to explain everything to you? Don't you speak English?"

"Fuck you!" Tony forgets my mother is watching. He loses it. He loses his English and sprays Joe with a string of stinking Cantonese curses.

Joe smiles, "Guess we're going to understand each other, then, old buddy." He leans forward to give Tony a friendly pat on the back, only from where he's sitting he can't reach, so he hits Tony on the knee, "So tell me, who sent you?"

"Whatchu talking about," Tony chops at Joe's hand.

Wap! — Joe almost knocks Tony's head off. Tony ends up mashed to one end of the sofa. "Bbbastard," he says after a while.

"Watch your language," Joe waves a thumb at my mother.

"Who gives a fuck! They're after me —"

Joe squints. He's trying to remember how he used to handle Tony. It's been a while.

"They're after me!"

Joe hitches his chair forward. He's caught the scent of desperation coming off Tony now, and like an old hound dog he runs after it, after the whiff of something familiar, something he used to smell, day in, day out. It clears his head. The smell of fear reminds Joe — the cop who hasn't touched his gun for two months, the cop told to dry out and clean up — it reminds him what he should be doing next. He lights a cigarette.

"You fff-king set me up," Tony grabs the cigarette from Joe and sucks on it. He sucks so hard he makes a popping sound when he pulls the butt off his lip.

"Fff-king set me up. You put the word out. You said I fingered Eddy," Tony's knee is bouncing up and down now, like a jackhammer.

"Where'd you hear this?"

"I heard it."

"Where?"

"I *heard* it."

"Tony," Joe lays a pack of cigarettes on the coffee table. "You can do better than that."

He pauses, he can hear my mother breathing at his back. "You can help us, or —" he lifts a shoulder. "It's up to you, chump. Isn't that right, Mrs. Wong?" Joe speaks to my mother without taking his eyes off Tony. My mother clears her throat.

"Mrs. Wong?"

"Mm?"

My mother moves her lips as Joe gets out of his chair. She doesn't know she's doing this, she's only trying to keep up with Joe. When he paces to the window and says,"Tony, you shit," she repeats, "Tony, you shit." She sits in her chair, back straight, eyes locked onto Joe. Nothing punctures the circle of light that ties her to the screen. Her face glows, her lips move; like the moon to the sun, she reflects everything that bounces out to her, and in this state she amplifies all that passes before her eyes.

"*You're* the one," Joe turns on Tony. "*You* cut out. Not me. We had a deal, remember? You get us Eddy, we take care of you."

"Eddy? Eddy?" my mother says.

"You haven't seen him yet," I tell her. "He's the dealer Joe tried to nail."

"For drugs, hmmm? I know, he's the bad guy."

"Yeah, but he got away."

"He did? Good, good."

My mother's getting the picture now; she doesn't need me anymore, she turns to Joe. "Hey," she kicks a leg out, "you going to make something happen?"

"Hold on," Joe replies. "I'm in the middle of something, Mrs.Wong. Aren't you following?"

He stops pacing and leans over Tony. "You," Joe says, "You drop out of sight. Nobody knows where. Nobody talks. Then all of a sudden you show up here. You break into my place. You say *I* put Eddy on your tail?" Joe leans further into Tony's face, "You're damn right I did! You had a deal with me, buddy." He grabs Tony's shirt and jerks him up.

"Stronzo!" he cuffs Tony on the head. Tony's neck snaps back. He bounces like a yo-yo on the sofa. Joe slams him in place, "Sit, goddammit."

Tony starts laughing, "Watch your language."

Joe has to step away. "Tony," he takes the rough stuff out of his voice now, "Tony. Listen to me. I don't have nothing for you. Not now. Not any more. You know that. What I had, I had to turn in. Evidence."

"Bullshit," Tony reaches for the cigarettes, but his hand trembles so much he knocks the pack to the floor. Joe kicks it away.

"How you going to score now? Suck up to Eddy? Do what he says? Is that it? Is that what's happening?" Joe grabs Tony by the jaw, "Who told you I set you up?"

"Nobody," Tony shakes his head free. "Nobody, goddammit."

"Nobody?"

"Nobody! Jesus! They just showed up, that's all. They showed up over at my sister's."

"Who?"

"Two guys. Regular guys."

"Regular guys?"

"Yeah, they do what they have to. They slap my sister around, then this other one comes in. He's the one smells. Not bad, but like he's going on a date, you know, and he says, 'Lady, don't forget. Tell Tony, this a message, personal, from Eddy.' "

"He said that?"

"What did I just tell you?"

"Lou said that."

"Yeah, Lou. It was Lou. Nobody smells nicer than Lou. Lou." Tony can't stop repeating the name. Under the sweat and junkie tremors, his mouth lifts in a smirk.

"Lou, the guy I told you to watch out for. The guy you shoulda shot when you had the chance. Lou," he waits for Joe to smack him one. But this time, it's Joe who flinches instead. A muscle on the side of his face twitches uncontrollably.

## II

Later that night, Tony sleeps on Joe's sofa. Joe paces his kitchen. And my mother sits before the two of them, shelling peanuts. She throws the shells into a bowl. The bowl is milky white, the night beyond a seamless black.

A lamp above my mother's shoulder throws a nimbus of light into her eyes. The glare makes it hard for her to see. She has to lean forward to find Joe on the screen in front of her. He's there — she can just make him out — the shadow following the glowing tip of a cigarette.

Joe paces to his kitchen sink. He hears something. His

cigarette hangs in mid-air. He jumps to the window. The streetlamp outside lights up half of his face, shadows plane away the rest. He takes a drink. The ice from the glass clunks against his teeth. He takes another drink.

Down below, the street remains empty. A lone car whooshes by, only to leave a backwash of silence so strong that it eddies out to my mother. She stops shelling peanuts. She listens. Nothing moves. Joe puts his glass down. He examines the shadows by each house, the bushes, the cars. He wants someone to step from that darkness and shoot him now, or he'll shoot himself, it's that kind of night. "Come on," he says. The streetlight blooms on his forehead. Black holes grow where his eyes should be.

"You okay?" my mother asks.

Joe doesn't answer. He pulls on his cigarette. He hears the refrigerator start up, the clock on the wall go tickticktickticktick. The sound makes his eyes twitch. He squints, trying to keep everything in focus, but the muscle in his jaw jumps suddenly, when a car comes from nowhere and advances down the street. Towards him. Slowly, slowing even more, the car stops just below his window. Without thinking, Joe does what he's done for ten years or more, he slides his window open and leans into the dark to greet his partner, "Hey," he says, "Frankie!" He smiles for the first time. My mother smiles along with him.

And the guy in the car below leans out his window to look up into the night. He sees Joe grinning from above. And behind Joe, on the other side of the screen, there's an old Chinese lady holding a bag of peanuts. She's showing him her choppers, too. "What's so funny?" Frankie says, "Let's go."

Frankie drives across town. Joe sits next to him in the front seat of the car. My mother settles back in her chair. The camera places her so she's looking right over Frankie's shoulder.

The night streams by. Streetlights throw their beams on the car, then fall away. For a while no one speaks, but something's bugging Frankie: he doesn't want my mother along. He looks at Joe.

"Mrs. Wong," Joe tells him.

Frankie looks in the rearview mirror. He moves his head until he catches the glow that's my mother's reflection. "Mrs. Wong," he says, "this is going to be tricky."

My mother doesn't respond.

"Can you understand me?" Frankie raises his chin and follows it with his voice, "Mrs.Wong?"

My mother moves around in her chair.

"You there?"

"Yeahyeah."

"You have to stay out of our way. You hear me?"

"I know," my mother's offended. "You don't have to tell me. I been watching Harry. All this time, *he* never complain about me." She shoves her back deep into her chair and takes a sip of tea. She's not going to budge, Frankie can see.

"Well, okay," he gives up arguing with her, "don't say I didn't warn you. Hang on."

He shoots the car down the street. Palm trees fly by. Houses. Street lights. Frankie's eyes take in the length of the road before him, its rise and fall, its center strip flowing by. With his foot on the gas pedal and one hand easy on the steering wheel, he could drive blind, he knows this road so well. He knows it will lead to the next road, and the next to the next, he can count on it, that's how things go, one road going into another, cars crossing, people meeting, who can stop the rush of roads intersecting, colliding. Frankie fixes his gaze on a traffic light up ahead.

Joe is still tight from hours of waiting by his kitchen window. He takes a deep breath and expels a night of drinking.

"Geez," Frankie pulls his head away. "Open the window, will ya? I thought you were cutting that out." He makes a sour face, "The captain's been talking, you know."

"What? About me?" Joe pretends surprise.

"Who else?"

Frankie lifts his face to the rear view mirror again. There's a glare in his eyes. My mother reaches up and turns her lamp down. "That better?" she says.

"Thanks," Frankie stretches in his seat. "Whatever you do," he says to Joe, "don't hang us up, okay?"

Joe looks at Frankie, "Hey —" but Frankie won't look back at him.

Frankie bangs the car across a set of railroad tracks. The front end tilts, the rear end scrapes the road, they climb a steep hill. Frankie and Joe ride up into a wide, dark sky. The silence of the night drops down on them. They've ridden through it many times before. Together in Vietnam, and now here. They respect the night. They have nothing to say until the car tips over the crest of the hill and the darkness of the heavens suddenly gives way to the glittering life below.

"Man," Frankie says.

"Shit," Joe's glad to have something to say, at last. "Can you beat that."

Frankie hangs the car for a moment over the jewel of a city, then he chunks it down the other other side of the hill. They sink into a long flat stretch and Frankie steps on the gas. He steers a straight line between the lights of the city on one side and the black nothing of the bay on the other.

"You ready for this?" he's smiling now, "It's gotta be peach."

"What?"

"The wedding. Sue wants peach. Peach cumberbunds. White tuxes. 'Cause it's summer," Frankie looks at Joe, "You know — you need something like that."

"Yeah?" A light shines on Joe's teeth, he's beginning to feel better. "If that's what you want, it's your show, Jack. Just don't put me through it more than once, you hear?" He takes a swing at Frankie, Frankie ducks.

They enter a park and pass into the dark reach of what lies before them, a curve of road, a black meadow. Everything they see now makes them sit up to scan the dark.

"Through the back," Frankie says.

"Tony drop it off?"

"Says he did."

Frankie drives out of the park into a cozy neighborhood. Rows of stucco houses and modest flats. At the end of a street anchored by a savings and loan, there's a cluster of small shops, all locked for the night: a bakery, a grocery, a five-and-ten. Discount clothes at the corner, coffee, and fish. Pet fish at the end of the block.

Frankie cruises the fish store. A light inside shows half the store seems to be given over to what looks like bookshelves. In the front window, a big sign says in Chinese and English, "Best Fish and Videos."

My mother can just make out the sign, "Hahh?" she says.

"Mrs. Wong —" Joe puts a hand up. He checks the street for suspicious-looking vehicles, creeping shadows.

"Keep your head down," he tells my mother. "Okay," he motions to Frankie.

Frankie clicks off the car lights and cuts into an alley behind the shop. Joe jumps out of the car. Frankie follows. They run down a short flight of stairs, push a door open, and bang into a dark room, their guns pointing.

A table of disemboweled fish lies before them. Two men back away from the fish with their hands up. Their palms shine white in the light from an overhead bulb. Little white packets drop from their hands.

Frankie flashes his badge. Joe flashes his. "Come on, come on," Frankie advances on the men. "Get it up."

Frankie throws one of the men against a wall of fish tanks. Joe throws the other. The water in the tanks slaps against glass. The fish, schools of goldfish and guppies, flare up in fright.

Frankie and Joe frisk the men. One of them tries to twist away. Frankie grabs his hair and shoves him into a wall of glass. "Well, if it isn't Eddy," he makes his voice thick and tired, "Ed-dy Chan. Whaddaya know. Got yourself another chump brother-in-law, huh?"

Frankie kicks Eddy's legs out from under him. Eddy slips, his skin squeaking down a wall of fish tanks. He falls to his knees.

The other man, the brother-in-law, looks away in shame. Joe puts handcuffs on him. "Eddy always uses his in-laws, so his own family stays clean," Joe tells my mother. "This one, this one's number three. Just got here."

"From Fuzhou? I know, they all coming from there now." My mother shakes her head. "Ehh," she talks to the brother-in-law in his own dialect, "Where you jump off the boat? You think you can come over here and do whatever you want? Just because you're here? Hahh? It's human, right?"

The brother-in-law pretends not to hear. He keeps his eyes on the floor.

"Bring him over here," Frankie says. He's already got Eddy handcuffed. He grabs the brother-in-law now and shoves him next to Eddy. "You look around," he says to Joe. "Let's go."

Frankie takes a bead on Eddy and his brother-in-law while Joe checks out the shop. The place smells like a gym, dank and sweaty. They're in a basement lined with fish tanks that burble and glow. The table is covered with goldfish gutted for the bags of dope in their bellies. Joe walks past the table and runs up a flight of stairs that leads to the shop above. He works fast. He shines a flashlight into an alcove under the stairs; it's filled with cardboard boxes. Joe rips into one. Porn videos. From Thailand. Hong Kong. And Shanghai.

"Shanghai?" my mother peers at the cover of a video.

Joe throws it down before she can check it out. He reaches for another. This one has a picture of a woman whose breasts are falling out over the titles. Joe grabs it and takes it over to Frankie.

"Looka this," Joe holds the video up for Frankie to see.

Frankie looks, but not at Joe.

"Miss Sukothai!" Joe waves the video. He took his R&R with Frankie in Bangkok. He wants Frankie to enjoy this one, too. "There you go," he shoves the video at Frankie.

Frankie looks over Joe's shoulder. There's something moving. Behind the boxes.

"Joe!" Frankie yells and a gun goes off. Bang into his eye. The eye that wouldn't look at Joe. The eye that saw something Joe missed. It falls onto Joe's shoulder and covers him with blood.

"Frankie! Frankie!" Joe pulls Frankie to the floor and brings up his gun.

My mother ducks. Eddy and his brother-in-law fly out the back door. But the guy behind the boxes comes out shooting. Joe drops behind the table. My mother slides all the way down in her seat; she crushes the peanuts she's been eating and scatters little pellets everywhere.

Joe shoots at the guy running for the door. Whump, whump, whump! Tanks of fish blow up. Big gold fish and little gold fish, fish with gorgeous tails, fish with priceless tumors on their heads, carp, tropical gems, gallons of water, shards of glass, pieces of castles, rocks, seaweed. The debris blossoms high and rains down on Frankie, Frankie dying on the floor. Bug-eyed fish flop off his face. Tiny iridescent ones swim in his blood. Joe can see a dozen mouths gulping for air.

Joe wakes, thrashing and coughing. He's fallen asleep in his chair by the kitchen window. The streetlight shines into his eyes. Now he sees my mother. She's facing him, her eyes full of compassion. And empathy.

My mother leans forward in her chair. Her face has become a reflection on her TV screen. She has turned her lamp up two notches to the 250 watts she needs to thread a needle, but at this setting the lamp throws her image straight onto the screen before her. Its light casts her into the kitchen along with Joe, and she only has to lean forward and her eye becomes Joe's eye, her thought his.

"You were dreaming," she says. "Dreaming."

"Ma'am —" He kicks his chair back. Peels his silhouette from my mother's reflection and rises to his full, lanky height. In three steps, he's at the kitchen sink. He turns on the tap, leaning into the cool metal of the sink, and stares at the water pouring out.

My mother watches him. She's patient, she understands. She knows what it's like to wake up in the middle of the night, not knowing how you have come to this moment in your life. When she had to work the late shift at the hospital, the three-to-eleven, she would get home at midnight, the tires of her car scrunching on the snow, the sound setting her teeth on edge, she would run for the house, her head aching from the cold, she would fall into a quick sleep in front of the TV, with her tea in her hand and her feet on a hot water bottle, she would drop off like this and the flickering light from the TV would write a stream of nonsense on her face: promos, jingles, the screams of late-night thrillers, all these washed over my mother as she slept, but soon — it varied from night to night, depending on the program — soon she would wake to the sound of a car crash or the cries of monster apes, Ahhhhee-AaaheeAhhh! She would jerk upright and spill her tea. Her mouth would be dry, her head still aching. She would get up and run to the sink as Joe does now.

"Spit it out," she says, "spit it out." She used to gargle with hot water, she was afraid of catching cold, she would gargle and spit out the bad dreams. "Boil water," she tells Joe. "Can you hear me?" She holds her breath. "Hahh? Drink something hot, then you feel better."

My mother waits for Joe to respond. He doesn't. He comes out of his stupor at the kitchen sink only to stick his head under the tap. He snorts and gags.

"Behind you," my mother says.

She startles Joe. He comes up swinging. Then he sees it's only my mother behind him, pointing to a dish towel.

"Mrs. Wong!" He grabs the towel and wipes his face. Returning to the kitchen, he takes up his seat by the window again. Now, he gives my mother his attention. She returns hers, undivided. They sit. Around them, the night presses close, but reveals nothing. In the room next to Joe, Tony still sleeps, undisturbed. His breath is loud and wet. He's a big dog keeping the night at bay.

In this stillness, Joe is a lone figure, lit just to the threshold of perception, Joe in his empty kitchen. The camera shows him in his solitude, then it dollies in slowly, it frames Joe in his chair at the window, it floats up his legs and past the armrests of his chair, it catches his hands taking out a cigarette, it closes in on his face, a match flares, his head moves to the flame, he sucks and the cigarette tilts up, red then gray, ashes growing on the tip. The camera moves in so slowly that my mother doesn't notice until she's right in Joe's face; the camera has dollied her in so close, she is staring now into Joe's eyes, they are gray and overcast; she is looking over the grainy surface of his skin, finding the deep line between his eyes tempered by the lucky mole high on his forehead; she is virtually intimate with Joe, the camera has pushed her so far, she can't help herself.

"Frankie!" she says.

Joe turns away.

"Frankie!"

Joe bends over to grope the floor. He pulls a shoe out from under his chair. A newspaper. An ashtray. He lifts the ashtray up and rolls the tip of his cigarette in it.

"How old was he?" My mother straightens her back. She's on the edge of her seat, working her lips, "How old?"

Joe drags on his cigarette, "A little older," exhaling, "than me."

"You?" my mother looks Joe up and down, "Forty. . . forty. . . ?"

He raises an eyebrow.

"Anyway, too young, ah?" She nods at Joe. To her surprise, he returns her expression of sympathy with an angry move; he stubs out his cigarette.

"No," he pushes his ashtray away. "He did a lot. In his life, Frankie did a lot. You don't even know!"

My mother stops talking. She can see Joe needs a break. She waits for him to go to the refrigerator and pull out a diet coke. Pop. Fizz. The coke transmits the reassuring sounds of the everyday. Joe lights another cigarette.

My mother resumes, she can't help herself. "Was he married?" she asks.

"Frankie?" Joe drops his match in the sink. My mother cocks her head. She makes Joe look away. "Almost," he says.

"Almost?" My mother purses her lips. She holds this thought for a moment, then she perks up. "Maybe he have children, hah? Children, anyway. With somebody he didn't tell?"

She sounds hopeful but she only makes Joe angry. "What're you getting at, Mrs. Wong? You trying to tell me something?"

"Oh no, I not telling you, I only asking. Your friend, he have family?"

"He had me. And his girlfriend. Is that what you want

to know?" Joe peels his cigarette off his lip. "Before Frankie got engaged, *I* was his family, okay? Me. I was the one. The only one. The only goddamn family Frankie ever had," he slams his hand onto the kitchen counter.

"Don't blame yourself," my mother says. "How can you know what will happen? Those guys —"

"I'm going to get them."

Joe paces to the window, my mother urges him on, "You have to —"

"Whatever it takes."

"You have to —" My mother transforms herself into the voice of hope, the voice of positive action. She knows what a story needs. On TV she has seen all the stories ever told. Her words draw Joe back to the camera. He stops with his eye pushed up to the lens.

My mother pulls back to see him better. Her glasses catch the light coming off the screen. For a moment, the bulge of her trifocals and the light glinting off their clumsy surface give a dotty cast to her face. She's given herself over to her infatuation with the screen. Her eyes have grown larger, her hair springs up white as dandelion fluff around her head.

"Joe," she says, "you have to do what you have to do. I know." My mother speaks to Joe now as if to herself. "For Frankie, for your family, there's no other way. You do what you have to — even it kills you."

She leans forward, she speaks what's in her heart, she pulls what she knows out of herself and gives it to Joe there on the screen; Joe, handsome and vulnerable; Joe, tall and troubled; Joe, clenching his jaw at her.

"Even it kills you, what can you do?" she cries into his face.

"Mrs. Wong —" he jerks away, surprised by my mother's sudden vehemence. Scared, almost, by her unsolicited outburst of passion; she's close to falling on top of him, leaning into her TV screen the way she is.

"Hold on," he says, "*I'm* the one. I'm going to take care of this for Frankie. Me and nobody else. You got that?"

Joe makes my mother back off. He puts his hands up as if to say, hey, how am I supposed to help you, and retreats to his kitchen window. There, he turns away from my mother and looks out once more into the night.

Left to herself, my mother sinks back into the wide arms of her chair. She's a small figure in a baggy brown vest. She sits looking at Joe, but it's hard to tell if she's still seeing him or something else. Her eyes have turned into ovals of glass. Is she looking out — the screen sends pulses of light across her face — or is she looking in? In on herself. A young self, as she was when she first came to this country, when she spent so many dark hours just like this, transported to some desolate place in her heart.

She is the one standing by the window now, she is the one just startled from her sleep, the one looking into the night. The wind gusts up and rattles the glass. Outside, the snow blows into steep drifts along the road, and beyond the road, high on a hill, the world is distilled into a field of snow. Thick to a stone wall and the sky above.

Looking out, my mother stands at her window and pounds her arms. Her shoulders, her bones. She aches from the cold. Every day she puts on her uniform, her white dress, white shoes, white stockings, she puts all this on in the reassuring light of day, yet when she looks in the mirror she shivers to see she's acquired a life not her own. Her life here is not her real life, it's just what she sees everyday. The seven-to-three and the midnight shifts. The cleaning, the washing. Her real life she left somewhere back in China, back before years of war changed everything.

Maybe in the school where the missionary sisters promised her a future serving God and the poor, maybe there where they taught her about germs and clean washcloths and gave her a mission to save all the women in China from death in childbirth, maybe there, in that school, in its whitewashed compound with students lined up in neat rows, a flag clanking to the top of a pole, the sun burning a bright spot on each forehead, the bishop intoning, maybe there she left not a memory shunted out of time but her real, true life, her life still whole and unwritten, thrown up before her with the wind, a haze of dust in the schoolyard, motes of things yet unnamed.

My mother stirs in the depths of her chair. When she was new to this country she used to spend a lot of time talking to the TV, practicing English. She practiced how husbands and wives talked to each other: "Hon, pass the butter, please. More potatoes, dear?" She practiced how kids talked to their parents: "Can I go to the game? Mom? Pleeeze." She learned the rituals of living here and searched the screen continually, dialing up and down the channels, chasing the spectra of sound and light, looking for the one thing that eluded her, a life she could claim as her own. Something more than the seven-to-three she put in at the hospital every day. Something better. Something big, even. Big as the dreams she'd had in school.

When she started learning English she used to ask people on TV if they wanted to trade their life for hers. "I give it to you free," she said. But no one ever stopped what they were doing — kissing their husbands, tucking their children in bed, making a joke, or backing their car out of the drive — to take her up on her offer. So now, now when she's old and knows better, she doesn't ask for so much any more, she doesn't. She just wants things to come out right. She wants to see justice done once in a while. If not in her everyday life, then in the pure realms of desire, in the moments when she clicks on the TV to see James Bond catapulted from a car or Dirty Harry blowing a guy away, she wants to see the world torn apart, bombed, shot, kicked, burned, beat up, brought to the brink, and then, cleansed of evil and ambiguity, restored to her, not as the drudgery of eight-hour shifts, but as a thrilling, infinitely repeating dream. For, if she cannot have her real life here, she can have this: my mother loves violence and she's ready for the next shootout.

"Ehh!" she leans from her chair now and talks to the TV in front of her. Everything there is dark. Joe is only a shadow again, moving by his kitchen window. My mother strains to see him. "Joe?" she reaches out a hand. "What you going to do now? What about the bad guys? Hahh? What about them?"

My mother punches up the brightness on her screen. She makes Joe turn from his window to look at her and as he does, the light from the street falls off the side of his face.

## III

With Frankie dead and Tony snoring in his living room, the parts of Joe's life come into focus. He sees now what he has to do: he walks across the room and throws a glass of water in Tony's face.

Tony wakes, snorting and cursing. He runs out into the night. Joe goes after him. This is what Joe has been planning all along, to track Tony the snitch, Tony the junkie going for his fix.

Tony crashes through the night streets to Chinatown, "What the fuck, what the fuck!"

He has to stop on a steep hill, he's out of shape. A kid who spent his life sitting on his butt, hiding in the rooms over the strip joint where he lived, his mother run off, his grandfather never talking. Tony with his crinkle hair and a face that didn't belong, a face created out of a nightclub romance and left for his grandpa to raise, a face the old man felt obliged to disown.

"Your mother like that, what I can do?"

The old man whipped the boy when he caught him playing pool. He stayed mad as hell to the day he died, falling from his barber chair before his morning shave, all the guys at Uncle's Cafe running from their breakfast waffles to stand and stare.

Tony hurls himself down the last hill to Chinatown. Joe follows, staying in the shadows.

My mother, in her chair, reaches for her cup of tea. She holds it in front of her, suspended between her and Joe, between faith and disbelief. "You going to do it?" she says, "Now?"

Joe slips behind a garbage bin. Across the way, Tony makes his move; he's heading straight for a noodle shop. He goes in, shoulders hunched, a big guy trying to look small.

From his spot, Joe has a good view of the place. He can see the shop is a shoebox, long and narrow, probably smelly, too. It glows in the green of fluorescent lights. Joe can make out a nice family inside. Two teenage boys and a woman who looks like their mother. They all have the same skinny build. One of the boys leaves with a container of noodles. The other disappears into the back of the shop. Only the mother is left, cleaning and mopping.

"Eddy's sister," Joe shakes his head. Damn. He sets her up in business and makes her husband run his contraband.

The woman barely looks up when Tony walks in. "We close," she says, and continues swabbing a mess off the floor.

"What's wrong her?" my mother sees the woman with her hair gone a rusted brown, her face, too. The woman's arms are as thin as sticks.

"Stop, stop," my mother puts her tea down to scold the woman. "Look what's going to happen to you. You don't stop working, you never see — aiya —"

Tony leans over the counter. "Lady," he says, "where's your husband?"

"Husband?" the woman looks mad at the word. She straightens up. "Who you?" She backs into the stove behind her. "What you want?"

"I gotta talk to YC."

"YC not here."

"I gotta talk to him."

"Go way!" the woman grabs the handle of a wok.

"Listen, lady, this a pickup. For Eddy, for chrissake."

"Winston!" the woman suddenly screams at the top of her lungs. A toilet flushes somewhere in the back.

"Winston!" the woman swings her wok at Tony. He grabs it just as the boy who disappeared into the back of the shop comes running.

"WINSTON!" the woman flies at the boy in a rage, "Why you gotta flush?" She slaps the kid in the face. "Don't you hear me? Hahh? Why you don't come?" She attacks the kid, "Flush toilet! Flush toilet!"

The woman pushes the boy into a chair. Tony drops the wok, rips open the cash register. It's empty. He slams his hand down. Toothpicks, chopsticks, everything on the counter goes flying, and soy sauce hits a little god sitting in his shrine. Black goo drips over the red statue.

"Anyway, they never clean him," my mother pushes her glasses up her nose. She's had enough of this woman and her nice family, "Workworkwork." What she wants is action. A line drawn in the sand. Two people walking toward each other. That's when you see that life has a purpose, not this workwork everyday, but a meaning reenacted before your very eyes: you live, you die.

"Okay!" my mother perks up as Tony escapes from the noodle shop. He cuts through Chinatown, dodging, slipping. Joe follows, a shadow Tony doesn't see. Tony's getting desperate for a fix, when — unh! — a hand comes out of the dark, and chops him down. My mother's eyes grow large. Tony keels over as Joe ducks out of sight, just in time.

When Tony comes to, he's propped against a wall. Across from him, a man sucks up noodles from a styrofoam container.

"Eddy!" Tony pulls himself up. He looks around. He's in Eddy's hideout, a room crammed with junk, the kind of stuff his grandfather used to collect, shoes and suits, cookie tins, dented hats. Piles of papers on the floor, faded girls shredding from the walls.

"Damn, this a new investment?" Tony turns to Eddy.

Eddy throws a packet of powder at him. "You want this, you come to me. Don't mess with my sister."

"Hey, man, I didn't do nothing."

"Shut up. Did I say you could talk to my family? You scared the hell out of my sister. Her husband don't work for me no more."

"No?"

"He don't have the guts," Eddy smiles. "Not like you."

He wipes his hands on a handkerchief. He's tidy. He jerks his wrists free of his shirt cuffs, then — wham! — he slams into Tony, knocking him over. Pulls him up — wham! — he knocks him into a wall.

"What the fuck you doing working for the cops?"

"I didn't do nothing."

"Shut up. Lou's the one shot Frankie, I didn't touch him. You tell that to Joe, your good buddy?"

"Who gives a shit?" Tony leers, "You're going to fry!"

Eddy lunges, Tony grabs him. The two men fall. Eddy tries to throttle Tony, but Tony rolls on top of him and jams a knee in — unh! — for every year he lived over the strip joint with his grandfather, he jams his knee in. For every meal he ate, the old man across from him, sucking up juk, pink teeth on a plate, for every needle stuck in his arm, for every lie told to his sister, every dollar taken from her, he pounds into Eddy now, a surge of adrenaline suddenly making him think he has all the power in the world, like everybody else in this big old country, all the power to get what he wants.

"Yeah," he flexes his muscles, he feels the bigness of everything rising in him now. "You're going to fry!" he slams into Eddy, "You're going to fry!"

Behind them — WHUMP — a wall explodes. "Aagh!" Tony rolls away in pain. A bulb swings overhead. It sends shadows across the room. A body steps out of the darkness, arm out, gun pointing.

"Joe?" my mother squints, but Tony already knows who's coming for him. He sees a gun and the hand holding the gun; it wears a fat jade ring. "Lou!" he chokes.

The gun comes down. Just as it's going to do what it's got to do — BAM — a bullet from across the room knocks the gun out of Lou's hand and sends it skidding across the floor. Eddy shoots back, wildly. Tony yells. Lou drops to the floor. And the guy who shot Lou? The guy who sneaked up on everyone? He jumps out of the room — BAM — Eddy hits the bulb overhead and throws the whole screen into darkness.

My mother stiffens in her chair. The only light now is the one behind her. It throws her image onto the screen. For a moment, all she can see is this: her reflection floating on the surface of the darkness, her head and a tremendous racket growing out of her head, a racket of bodies crashing into walls and falling down stairs. Three bodies tumbling from Eddy's hideout into an abandoned lot.

"Lou," my mother counts the bodies falling out, "Eddy. Aaand —" she sees the shadow not yet accounted for, "Joe! I knew it!" She turns the volume up.

WHING, a bullet shoots past her nose and decapitates a bush. Lou leaps from the bush and runs, diving behind a pile of junk.

"Get him, get him," my mother pokes a finger at the screen, all thought of life's purpose gone. You live, you die.

"Mrs. Wong! Joe flattens himself against a wall. "Get outta here," he runs from my mother.

She brings her finger down, "Joe." Her chin goes up.

Joe works his way to where Lou is hiding. Lou waits, gripping his gun. "Joe. Listen to me. Hey, Joe —"

"Pipe down," Joe brings up his gun. "You want the cops to come?" He stretches his lips, not grinning at his own joke, but getting ready to do what he has to do. He creeps to a shed near Lou.

"Listen," Lou shouts, "If I woulda known, I wouldna done it. Not to Frankie — you hear me?"

Joe jumps out and shoots.

A crazed giggle comes back at him, "Jesus, man. Whaddaya want? I just told ya. I wouldna done it if I woulda known!"

Joe presses his head into the side of the shed. My mother can see only his jaw sticking out.

"Come on, Joe," Lou peers from his pile of junk. "Look at it this way. I'm in the cellar with Eddy and his fuckin' fish. Eddy's too cheap to put in more lights, so how'm I supposed to know it's a coupla my friends come through the door?"

WHING. Joe shoots again.

Lou hits the dirt. When he comes up, his face is grimy, his giggle gone. His craziness takes over. "Jesus!" he spits junk out of his mouth, "I was only doing what I had to!" he yells. "You the one fucked up, Joe."

Behind Lou, Eddy circles the yard. "Careful, careful," my mother says.

She sees a bit of Joe, off to the side, just the glint of an eye. Whing! Whing! Lou and Joe exchange shots.

Eddy slides by them. He races for the street, ducking, jumping. Lou sticks his head up. He sees something dark getting away, and he shoots. Bam, bam! Eddy leaps up and drops like a rabbit.

Lou races to him, "Joe!" he says and suddenly he gets it in the chest. His hands fly up.

Joe runs to him, gun cocked, feet stepping over blood. He drops to his knees. His eyes flinty, his pact with Frankie not yet finished. He puts his gun to Lou's head. My mother squeezes her eyes shut, Lou opens his — and then the sirens come, screaming through the night.

## IV

Later, after the bodies have been disposed of — Eddy and Tony sent to emergency, Lou to the morgue — my mother waits for Joe to finish with a police detective. The medics have already left, their lights flashing. The police go now. So do the gawkers. Only the detective keeps a hand on Joe. He's talking about Lou. He taps his chest.

"Looks clean. Got him coming at you, I'd say," he studies Joe. "We'll take care of this. You need a ride home?"

"Thanks," Joe sticks out his hand, "I'll walk."

Joe lets the detective drive away. When the street is quiet, he leaves the place where his life has acquired a new distinction, a weedy lot now bound by yellow police tape. He walks with his head down, the camera tracking him and my mother following wherever the camera leads.

She's as pensive as he is. When she sees murder and mayhem on the screen like this, something opens in her, deep and unpredictable, a vein of feeling, of memory and desire. All the things she can't express when she works seven-to-three. Things she would like to tell Joe now.

He turns a corner.

Things like fear and loneliness, things that used to keep her up half the night, watching people shoot each other so there would be nothing left to shoot.

"I was scared," she says.

Joe enters an alley, tall houses cutting off the space above; only one light shines up ahead. My mother follows, giving herself over to the darkness on the screen before her, going into that vein of memory opening from the past.

She follows Joe through the alley and comes out the other end, still thinking. Thinking of the time some thirty years ago when she was new to this country, new to the hospital where she was working, new and scared.

She went to change a bed in the maternity ward one day and found a woman there, a woman like herself just starting a life in America. "She was Mrs. Chu," my mother remembers now, "the second wife of the second son — the first wife died — of the deputy assist police chief. From Nanping. Important place, that woman tell me, but who ever hear about it."

"What?" Joe turns to look at my mother. He sees only the glare coming off her glasses on the other side of the screen. "This way," he walks down a dip in the road.

"I didn't know that woman and she didn't know me, but she grabbed my hand and she said, 'Please. Don't tell my husband! Hide this for me!'

"Like that, she gave me her money. Can you believe? Six hundred dollars!"

Joe comes to a low wall. The hill drops away and the water lies beyond, an expanse of black with lights winking in the distance. Beyond the lights a faint gray shows where the black is beginning to concede a horizon. To the right, the night retains its sparkle: a span of lights crossing into the dark.

"The bridge," Joe says, "Look."

My mother sits forward in her chair. She looks at the bridge, the water, and the night turning into day; she can see such a distance now.

Holding that woman's money, smelling the sour smell of milk coming off her, she wanted to run away that day. Away from the hospital. She wanted to go home. Return to her real life. Running on the riverbank when she was a child, watching the village women wash clothes. The pigs rolling in the mud. The boy herding ducks. A shirt smacked on a big rock.

She liked to watch from high on the riverbank. The sun climbing out of the river. She would chew sugarcane and spit it out. All around her feet, she littered the ground. When her amah finally came rushing up, breathing ragged and shouting in a big loud voice, she threw her sugarcane away and let the amah lead her home.

"Where do you think you're going? Hahh? Do you even think? A girl like you, where can you go?" The amah yelled all the way back.

"Her feet hurt," my mother says.

"Sorry," Joe looks out at her. "You want to get going?" He turns down a flight of stairs.

"I wanted to run," my mother continues. "From that room, from the hospital. But the woman there, oh, she won't let go."

She pushed her money at my mother. My mother pushed back. They struggled, Mrs. Chu bouncing on her bed, my mother swatting her down. Each tried to be more polite than the other.

"No —"

"Please —"

"No —"

As if the money they were fighting over were a real gift, and one too generous to be accepted.

They tore at each other until the woman dug into my mother's arm and held on. Her fears fell out of her then, with the hairpins knocked loose from her head. Her fear of a husband who beat her, her fear he would find out she was keeping money for herself, her fear of putting her money in a bank, her fear of losing this money and maybe her husband, too, bad as he was, who else did she have, she didn't want to be abandoned in America, wandering the streets, no one talking her language, no one knowing where she came from, if it was going to be like this, she would be better off back in China, even with the communists — all the woman's fears popped out of her with her hairpins, they hit my mother in the face, the arms, the eye.

My mother spit out the hairpins and tried to sit on the woman. The woman threw her off. She ripped into my mother's uniform, begged and cried, "How can I live here, how, how, how?" She begged until at last, my mother ran from her room with her money.

Later, my mother was careful to count the six hundred dollars to make sure every dollar was there. She wrapped the money in a clean cloth and kept it safe until the woman had to leave the hospital. In this way, she was able to account, exactly, for the portion of life's terrors that the woman had pushed on her.

"Four days!" she shakes her head, remembering. "And I'm only one can take care of that woman because I'm only one speak Chinese. I'm lucky, ah? After her, I learn lot. I know better. I just do what I have to do. I don't think about before, what's so good. I don't think about now, what's so bad. I don't think, is this my life, or is it somebody else? After I see that woman, so crazy —"

My mother rolls her eyes, lifts her chin, she's a Chinese opera star getting ready to hit her high note, the cymbals behind her going bongbongbongbongbong.

"After I see *her*," she says, "I don't *dare* worry any more! You know, Joe?"

She looks at Joe on the screen. He turns. "Sure," he smiles at her. "We're almost there."

He steps off the flight of stairs and goes left. A wind sweeps down the street and chills his face. He pulls up his collar, walks on, down another hill, the camera pulling back, rising, showing him going into a street of tall buildings, his life growing large and dark around him, the city opening up, all glass, brick, and stone, and high above, the sky growing pale with morning light.

Joe stops in a narrow doorway. My mother's eyes go

bright with curiosity. "This your place?" she asks.

Joe nods. He jingles his keys, not sure whether he should invite my mother in or not.

"Oh," my mother gets embarrassed, realizing his predicament, "No, no, you better go. Go rest. Please," she waves Joe towards his door.

Joe brings up his hand, as if to lift his hat to my mother, but since he doesn't have a hat, he salutes instead, and with the light over his door bouncing off the back of his head, and a morning haze, blue-gray, touching the side of his face, the merest touch, he says, "Well. It's been a pleasure, Mrs. Wong.

All process scientific
original vitamins sucrose
mineral 60 percent
colour and flavor
fresh like.

Hygienic, nutritious and easy to prepare
ideal for soup
making refreshing delicious
put dehydrated cole in water
boil as usual to make soup
not as unusual.

Before cooking together with meat
not apart
put dehydrated cole in hot water
till it fully absorbed
then pick it up and chop it to pieces.

SO PLAIN, SO EASY to cook. Crinkly packs of dirty dried cellulose. Sixty-five cents for 5.29 oz. Instructions for ingesting written in pale English and Chinese on the back. This is what the China National Native Produce and Animal By-products Import & Export Corporation Hunan Branch has caused to be shipped to the corner of Broadway and Stockton within sight of our glorious silver-spanned bridge.

Oh, brief of dehydrated cole: on a dark day, you cure everything.

# BELTWAY

WHEN MY FATHER DISAPPEARED into the great loop of the Washington, D.C. Beltway, his day started off like any other day. He got up, went to the kitchen, split a bagel in half and dropped his breakfast into the toaster. He had two plates out and a tub of margarine already opened by the time my mother walked in on him.

"You forgot," he said.

"What?"

"The bagels."

"Oh."

My mother went to the counter and poured coffee. She mixed in milk, added sugar, and was giving my father his cup when the toaster popped. "There's your bagel," she said. "What you complaining about?"

"You forgot."

"No, I didn't. They're here."

"Yes, but yesterday. What about yesterday?"

"What about?"

"They weren't."

"Aiyaa," my mother started for the door. She took her coffee with her.

"They were in the freezer!" my father called after her. "Good thing, I took them out. Otherwise, today. Today, what do we have to eat!"

He sat in the kitchen and listened to my mother go through the house. He tracked her footsteps across the floor, the silence when she reached the carpet, the creak at the top of the stairs, the last creaks at the bottom, the door opening, the sounds of the day buzzing in.

"Close it," he yelled. The door banged shut. He returned to his breakfast and stabbed the toaster with a fork.

I can see him now, pulling his bagel out. He'll do it slowly, so it won't tear. He'll scrape on margarine, add jam, take a bite. His nose will wrinkle, his jaw work overtime. "Tough," he'll push his plate aside, thump the bagel he still has left to eat. He'll tell himself — one more time — he shouldn't buy bagels any more, not on sale at any rate.

He'll pull a napkin from the napkin dispenser, wipe the table in front of him. Under his elbows. He can't stand a crumb out of place, papers dropped any which way. He'll clamp his mouth shut, his blood pressure will go up. He'll remind himself: everything has a place and everything in its place. This is how he lives, if he didn't, where would he be now?

Something rattles by outside. My father looks and sees his neighbor pushing a big blue garbage can up the drive.

"Mr. Lew," his neighbor notices him, "you know about Wednesday?"

"Chuh, Chuh," my father waves through his screen window.

The neighbor, the first to introduce himself when my parents moved to their new house — "Don't call me Peter, Pete's good enough" — stops now to figure out what my father has just said. He can't understand how my father still talks the way he talks after thirty years in this country. Pete has raised a family and retired on the easy cadences of his native Virginia. He has never had to budge a vowel, drop a verb, change when he didn't want to, change tenses, change a life. Pete has rarely, if ever, had to conjugate a circumstance other than the one he already knows.

When he first met my father, Pete said, "You need help, just holler."

My father said, "Holler?"

Pete walked over to his kitchen window and stuck his head out to demonstrate.

After that, my father thought Pete was pretty funny. So did my mother. She and my father set up the kitchen in their new house and, as soon as the wok was in place and the fryer plugged in, they made eggrolls and delivered these, hot, to Pete and his wife next door.

"What's that, Mr. Lew?" Pete pauses in the middle of his drive now, as my father calls out to him. He hoists up his garbage can, his nose in the air.

"Chuh, Chuh."

Pete looks away. Down the row of azaleas he has planted the length of his drive. "Ahh," he sniffs it out, "Chuck! Chuck! Sure, Chuck. Yeah. Don't forget."

"What?"

"The clean-up. Next Wednesday. They'll take your old paint and thinner. Whatever you don't want, put it out there."

Pete waves and disappears into his house. His place is identical to the one my parents have just moved into. A split-level with a small lawn in front and a bigger lawn in back. Pretty trees and shrubs all around. My father's glad he sold his business and retired here. The neighborhood is neat and clean, not like his old place with shopping malls going in where good houses used to be. My father's quite happy with his new home, only he misses a few things about the old, and chewing the tough bagel that morning reminds him; he puts his plate in the sink.

My mother doesn't hear him leave. She is in the back yard, overwhelmed by the bugs that have come to eat her newly planted roses. Only Mrs. Macomber watches as my father backs down his drive. She stands at her window and does not move until he slides off the curb and into the road. She is not going to let him run over her lawn any more. Her lawn extends down to his drive; his drive does not extend onto her lawn. "It doesn't work that way," she has told him several times already.

He goes left at the light, right at the church, and left again. Then, before the cars merging from the right cut him off as they move left to the middle lane leading to the mall, he moves right one lane, lets a car go by, moves right another and, following a van muscling its way through, pops out of the mess of merging cars to find himself rolling free at last, onto the Beltway. The entrance is clear.

My father hasn't been on the Beltway since he moved. Even then, he negotiated that trip only with the help of my mother, "Go right. Go left." My father does not go any distance without my mother at his elbow. He needs those extra eyes to read signs, to focus the English at fifty-five miles an hour. He needs the voice telling him, though he wishes it weren't so sharp:

"Right. Right. Four-nine-five, right. Two mile. One mile. Get over. Half. Get over. Yah, after this — go, mister, go — he's letting you. Go —"

"Who?"

"Go!"

"Who?"

"Who is in this car! Ai, you missed it!"

"You didn't tell me."

"I told you."

"You told him! Not me. How I know you talking to

me? Go, go, go! You want me hit that guy?"

My father has not ventured any distance from his new house yet. In the three weeks since he moved, he has only driven a few blocks to the supermarket and the drugstore. He knows it's all left turns going one way and right turns coming back. He has found Giant's and Safeway and CVS Drugs and a donut shop he should not go to. He feels reassured because — unlike the old country, where moving often means losing everything — here, all the stores come with you; they not only come, they remind you that they're still with you, next door, your friend, your neighbor. My father enjoys the ads and the mailers he gets every week. He, who once spent a month riding the rails in China to find a school, to find a sister, to escape the bombing, he's glad to have no more to do now than to go down the street and pick up milk at the supermarket, blood-pressure pills at the drugstore. My father likes routine. Establishing habits. These fix the landscape. Tell him what's happening. If he goes to buy milk at nine, and he goes to Giant's, then, at nine he always knows where he is going and for what. Over the years, my father has developed his own kind of compass.

He finds the spot on the Beltway that he likes. It's not the first lane on the right, that's for slowpokes. Nor the two to the far left, they're for people asking for traffic tickets. He settles on the second lane from the right; police don't get you here, his son has told him.

He's surprised at how everything has turned out. So simple, really. Here he is, on his way, going past green fields. And trees. And shiny glass towers.

My father settles into his seat. He has clip-on sun glasses and a baseball hat, Red Sox, because his son is a Red Sox fan. On the seat next to him is a shoebox he has outfitted with a section for a paper pad and pencils and another section, further subdivided, for nickels, dimes, and quarters. He's ready to pay his toll from here to anywhere, though he's lucky this time, from here to Washington he doesn't have to pay a penny, he can sail right through. At this rate, he'll be home before my mother knows he's gone. He should have told her when he left. Usually, he does. Usually, he shouts up the stairs so she can hear, "I'm leaving, ah!"

"Four-nine-five," he reads a sign coming at him. *North.* Is it north? To where he's going? College Park? My father can name the exit to his old place and he'll recognize it when he gets there. But until then, he can't remember, is it north from here?

Another sign goes by. He can't read the exits fast enough now. He's beginning to think he should have brought my mother along. He knows he has to go around Washington before he gets close to College Park. When he bought the new house, he moved from one side of Washington to the other, east to west. That much is clear. He's not confused over the thousands of dollars he paid to move in the right direction. To get back to his old place, he should be going the opposite way, west to east. So now, why is the freeway not following the obvious reasons for which it was built — to take people from one side of the city to another and connect them to all the possible directions in which they might go? Why is this one resisting clarification?

My father sees more numbers up ahead. This has to be it. Even if he's going north, not east, it has to be he's on the right road. Four-nine-five *is* the Beltway, after all. Yah. His son has told him many times, "Think of it like a donut."

"Donut?" Why does his son have to talk to him like he knows nothing? "How about bagel?" he says.

His son looks at him, "Okay, bagel. Whatever. Donut, bagel, just remember, the Beltway goes around and Washington's the hole."

My father makes a face at his windshield. Is it the sun? Or is it his son? His son's the one always giving him a headache. "It's the concept, Dad. If you'd just get the concept, then you'd get it."

"Get what? Get a donut? I want a donut, I go *buy* one. Why I need to *think* about it? What for?"

My father pulls down his sun shade. Whatever they learn, your kids will beat you over the head with it. What can you do? You keep going. Is it supposed to be north? Or south? Who knows. Who knows what the government does, they just put up a sign and you follow it. Anyway, if the Beltway goes in a circle, as long as he gets on and keeps driving, sooner or later he'll get where he wants to go. In the meantime, he just doesn't know where he is, exactly.

He starts looking for landmarks, the river first. He has to cross the Potomac. Here, it's Virginia, over there Maryland. He has to cross to the Maryland side pretty soon. If he gets to Maryland, that means he's doing okay, he's still going *around* Washington, which is what he wants to do. To go *into* Washington is to end up going the wrong way forever. My father knows.

Last year, on one of his rare trips into the city, he took a guest to eat dim sum in Chinatown. The guest was the grandson of an old professor of his. The boy was twenty-two, old enough to know what's what, my father said. Old enough to know better, my mother replied. The boy had just come from China to start college here. He was staying for the summer with my parents in their old house.

My father drove the boy into Washington and somehow as they were crossing the Mall, the boy looked to his left and saw the Washington Monument at the far end. My mother, seeing what he saw, and seeing how pretty the sun was shining at that moment, thought what a good picture it would make to show everyone in Kwangtung, with the boy smiling at the monument. "You cannot get that thing and him all in one picture," my father told her, but my mother, ignoring him, said, "Go straight," so my father went straight and, waiting for my mother to tell him what next, he drove the length of Independence Avenue until Independence all of a sudden gave out, and before he knew it he was swept up in the undertow of Fourteenth and heading straight for the bridge over the Potomac. When he came to and jammed his foot down, his car, old as it was, kicked into overdrive, bouncing him into an exit and delivering him, somehow, to the Jefferson Memorial. Once there, though, he was no better off, for he had to find a road to get out, and the road he found only led to — what else? — another memorial.

On the Beltway now, my father crosses the Potomac without realizing he has crossed. It's only when he climbs a hill that he thinks to glance back, but by then the river's already gone. He has to start looking for other landmarks.

Years ago, when he first came to Washington, he would never have thought the best route was the one on the outside, circling. No, like everyone else, he thought you had to go for the center, for State, the Voice of America, Commerce, Agriculture, the Library — he wanted to work for the government. That's what he would have done in China, so why not here? If his English wasn't as good as an American's, you had to admit, his Chinese was better. Maybe someone could use his Chinese.

"CIA," a nice boy in the congressman's office said. "They use all kinds of people."

"What can you do for us?" the CIA man said when he got there. The man didn't seem too interested, but he took out a pen.

"Crop analysis," my father said.

"Crop analysis?"

"Yes, rice, vegetables. I collect data. For Canton."

"The province?"

"Yes. It's difficult. Very."

"What is?"

"Collecting data. My bank, we need the best, you know. All kind of information so we can make loans."

"Loans?" The CIA man suddenly woke up. "Are you telling me you made loans? In China? Under the communists?"

The man grilled my father up and down. He warned about lying to the government. My father protested he wasn't lying; he was only talking about what he used to do.

"*Used* to do?" the CIA man became insulting. "We're talking about now, sir. Now. Not then."

"That's what I'm talking about, too," my father could get just as belligerent, "I'm talking about now, like you. Before, what I used to do, I want to do now. That's why I'm here. You see?"

The CIA man suddenly shut his mouth. He stared at my father and tapped his pen. Then he disappeared. It wasn't until later when my father talked to a friend, that he realized he hadn't been interviewed for a job at all. He'd been debriefed.

"Jefferson, Lincoln, Lincoln, Jefferson."

The third time my father circled those monuments with the professor's grandson, my mother suddenly went crazy and shouted at him. He pulled over. The boy from China who was sitting in the back seat jumped out and threw up. Right by Lincoln. In front of all the marble and the tourists. The boy wasn't used to cars. My father said, "That's okay. Stand still." He snapped pictures of the boy, anyway. "We are here, aren't we?" he said to my mother. She gave the boy one of the mints she always carried in her purse. My father stamped his feet, took a couple more pictures when the boy could muster a smile.

"Ready?" my father waved the boy and my mother back into the car. He drove carefully, avoiding the wrong turns he had made earlier, and found his way back to the Mall.

From there it was an easy ride to Chinatown and the best dim sum restaurant the city had to offer.

My father ordered siu mai, ha-gau, fen gau, cha-shau bao, ma-tuan, chang-fen, pai-gu, luo-bo gau, yu-tou gau, guo-tieh, chun-zhuan, nuo-mi, dan-ta, and two plates of noodles.

"People come here and think we have everything," he told the boy from China. "They don't see, it's not so easy."

"English, English," he tried to pass on what he had learned, "The most important thing. Number one. You don't sound American, they don't treat you American."

My father spoke in Chinese, but even so, the boy didn't pay attention. He looked at his food, looked away, looked down, looked away. He had recovered quickly from the car ride. He liked the spareribs best and built a pile of little bones on his plate. My father said later that the boy was shifty-eyed. My mother said, "No, he's looking at the girls. Next table. You don't see?"

She thought the boy was cute. My father said, "Cute? He look like Tiananmen, that one."

"The one in pajamas? That's cute."

"Cute! If I put on pajamas and yell at the prime minister I be cute, too! Chee —"

My father has no patience for the young people coming from China these days. "They think they suffer and we have so much. They think we owe them something. But they don't know, they have it easy. When we come here, nobody give us anything. We cook and clean. And they? They put on pajamas — wah, they're big heroes."

He almost accelerates into the car in front of him. He has to pull left, then left again to avoid hitting a semi. A little white car cuts in front of him. It has come from nowhere just to give him trouble. He moves another lane to the left, and so does the white car. He moves back. The darn thing stays in front of him like a fly mashed to his forehead.

He reaches for his radio. "Maybe Bach, maybe Beethoven." He tries to calm down. But the little white car sticks to his head, and so does the thought of that boy from China.

The boy saw how my father lived — in the old house with the new mall growing in the back yard. He saw the car my father drove, a clean but old Buick. He saw the business my father had, a restaurant called Ah Fong's with its name and eggroll specials acquired from the previous owner. The boy saw and remembered that his grandfather in China had said, "Mr. Lew, I taught him economics." The boy added up two and two, went north to college, and within the year, married his landlady.

"How old? How old? Chinese, too?" my mother dug up the details. My father wrote the letter that had to be sent to China.

"What a mess!" he whips through a curve in the Beltway. "Lousy no-good-for-nothing boy —"

Up ahead, he notices a new number, ninety-five.

"Hah?" he pulls off the road. The Beltway should be *four*-nine-five. What is this? He looks back. There it is. The Beltway has split in two. One road going one way, and the other, the other. He is on the other, the new route split from the old.

My father puts his car in reverse. He waits for the road behind him to clear, then, keeping to the shoulder, he backs cautiously down to the Beltway, straight into the highway patrol.

My brother is the one who gets the call, around eleven, from Officer Baker. Officer Baker says, "We have a Chuck here. Chuck Lew — what? — hold on —"

My brother hears the officer pause as someone talks to him at the other end.

"Hello," the officer gets back on the phone. "He says he has a hat."

"A hat?" my brother says. "What's going on?"

"Here —"

There's a clunk and my father comes on the line "The hat you gave me, okay? Red Sox!"

"Okay, okay. Calm down. Why're you telling me this?"

"Why? So you know! I'm me! "

There's another clunk and the officer gets back on the line.

"Don't you have his license?" my brother is getting angry.

"You bet."

"What's wrong then?"

"His driving."

"His driving?"

"Yep. You want to come get him?"

"I can't, I'm working. What's going on? Can't you just point him in the right direction? He'll make it. Nothing wrong with his eyes."

"I'm not talking about his eyes. I'm talking about his driving. Tell him how to drive."

The officer puts my father back on the phone. My brother tells my father, "He wants you to go only one way on the freeway."

"I don't go any way except one way one time."

My father nods at the officer as he hands back the phone. The officer talks some more with my brother, then my father puts his hat back on his head. "Red Sox," he points his thumb up. A half hour later, he's released, back to the Beltway.

He drives now, both hands gripping the steering wheel; he doesn't want any more trouble. He goes up a rise. And suddenly the Mormon temple is before him, floating over the freeway. Immediately, it gives him a sinking feeling. If he's going east on the Beltway, he should see three spikes, if he's going west, he should see five. If this is five, this is west and he's going the wrong way. The police tricked him! Must be. His son must have told them to point him home, but he wants to go the other way, east.

My father gets off the Beltway and searches for something familiar. Maybe a McDonald's. It's past noon already; he's starved.

He orders a fish sandwich, fries and a milkshake. When his food arrives, he retreats from a crowd of jumping children and finds a quiet table. Next to him, an old man cries over his Big Mac. The man wipes his eyes; his face flushes a deep pink.

"Hay fever," he apologizes.

My father sits down. "Cold's no good," he volunteers, "for you."

The other man looks puzzled.

My father points to the man's drink.

"This?" The man holds up his cup. "It's just coke."

"That's what I mean." My father squirts ketchup on his fries. "It's cold."

"Oh." The other man looks at his drink and rattles the ice. "I can't stand their coffee, that's why. You ever had their coffee?"

My father bites into his sandwich.

"It's terrible. Always burns my mouth." The man closes his eyes, blinks.

"Milkshake," my father says.

"Huh?"

"Milkshake."

"Nah, it's coke, I'm drinking coke."

"Yah, but ish better," my father can't talk for the food in his mouth.

"What is?"

"Milkshake! Ish better than their coffee."

"Hell," the other man's eyes fill with water. "So's the coke." He sneezes.

After lunch, the hay fever man points my father in the right direction. As he waves goodbye, he squints his big pink face to shout, "Ah Fong's, huh?"

"Sweet and sour, shrimp fried rice!"

My father toots his horn and he's on the freeway again. If he didn't have to work so hard to figure out where he was going, he could take it easy, couldn't he, just like all these Americans, order deep-fried wonton. With plum sauce. He eases his belt and settles back.

Meanwhile, at home, as the lunch hour passes, my mother, worried now, glances one more time at the kitchen clock and goes to the phone to call my brother. "Where is he?" she complains. "His noodles are waiting."

When my father arrives in College Park, the first thing he does is drive by his restaurant — he still thinks of it as his. He wants to see if the new owners have changed anything. Nope — they've done just what he did when he bought it. Add a coat of paint and ignore the name, "Ah Fong's."

"Ah Fong's" is written out in a swish of red on one of those freeway-readable signs. It rises high, and at night its name glows while little white lights chase around the edges. Underneath, where Frank would be billed at the Sands, or Wayne at the Flamingo, it's "Buffet All You Can Eat!" at Ah Fong's.

My mother said she never came to America for this. My father said, "What you talking about, this *is* America."

He left the sign alone because it cost too much to tear it down. The new owners, he can see now, have come to the same conclusion. "Ah Fong's. Lunch buffet. All you can eat." My father reads the sign as he drives by, "Diet Delight" — what's that?

He slows down to ponder the menu and to count the cars in the lot. So-so. He used to do better, but then, maybe it's just today. Today, it's after lunch already, and the insurance office there, they consolidated, so a few hundred people less, then the bank moved. Good thing he sold when he did. Before everybody left.

My father pulls into a strip mall. He has to remove his hat and swat his shoulders before he will allow himself to get out of his car. He walks the length of the mall, past hair, nails, and pizza to a window where a jade plant shares a space with sacks of rice.

*Beep.* He steps through a door into a long, dim shop. Something rustles in back. A woman appears.

"Mr. Lew! How are you? "

"Mrs. Ma."

"My. How's the new house?"

"Good, good."

"And Mrs. Lew?"

"Good, good."

"Goodness!"

My father and Mrs. Ma run out of the easy things to say. Fortunately, she's got a hammer in her hand; my father addresses this, "What are you doing?"

"Oh, you don't want to know," she shows him. "This shelf. Guess what happen? The boy he bring the soda? Look, how he knock it over. These days," she switches to Chinese, "You cannot get good help."

"Let me see."

My father spends the next two hours fixing Mrs. Ma's shelf. He stays on his knees hammering and leveling, one shelf turns into two, and pretty soon he's shoring up the whole section where Mrs. Ma keeps her soy sauce and chilis.

"Don't do this," she protests. "My son, he's home next week. He'll do it," she goes to wait on a customer.

My father finishes his job. He stands and cracks his knee. He's getting too old for this, really, but when he sees something broken or unfinished, he has to fix it. He has to square corners and straighten aisles. He has to go from shelf to shelf and brace the canned goods, label out, for their proper inspection. Whenever my father sees something out of place, the noise of everyday that clutters his mind and confuses his ears, people saying this and that, phones ringing, salesmen arguing — I owe you? You owe me! — all this buzzing, whizzing, this English fades away, and he sees at once what it is he has to do.

He picks up the nails, sweeps the floor. When he's done, Mrs. Ma hurries over and pats the shelves. "Mr. Lew," she says, "you *are* an engineer! "

"Economist, economist —"

My father does not mind Mrs. Ma getting his profession wrong, who knows about it anyway. What makes him take a step back is her enthusiasm. She's too energetic. Smart. Running this place all by herself after her husband passed away.

"You worked so hard, you must have something to eat. Come," Mrs. Ma leads my father to a back room where she has a card table laid with tea and cookies.

"Ice cream?" she says, "I have ice cream, too."

"Oh no."

"Don't be polite now. I know you like it. Vanilla? Chocolate?"

"No, no. Thank you."

Mrs. Ma serves my father a plate of cookies and two mounds of ice cream. He's getting tired. And he's afraid — it's late already, too late. He should be calling my mother, but he knows she will ask where are you and she will get him to say, I am with Mrs. Ma, but this won't be enough and she will get him to say, further, I am eating ice cream with Mrs. Ma.

"How can I finish this," he says. "You have to have some, too."

Mrs. Ma shakes her hand. "I don't dare. My daughter says too many calories."

"To you?"

"Oh yes, I have to watch myself, you know. We are all getting old," Mrs. Ma laughs.

"You? No, no, impossible."

My father spoons up ice cream before he realizes he

has said something not so correct; he has never before commented on anything personal about Mrs Ma, she is too good looking. But now? Now he has ice cream on his face.

Mrs. Ma pretends someone has entered the store. She goes out for a moment, though the front door hasn't beeped. My father quickly finishes his ice cream, enough of it so he can leave the rest to melt, politely, into its dish.

When Mrs. Ma returns, she has become quite serious. She says, "Mr. Lew, we're old neighbors, aren't we? We can talk."

"Of course." My father pushes his chair back. He would like to leave now, but Mrs. Ma hitches her chair closer as he pulls his away.

"You won't think me too — you know —"

"Mrs. Ma —"

"No, no, this is something, really, I need help with. It's my son."

"Your son?"

"Yes. He's applying to medical school."

"Medical school?"

"Yes. But there is a problem. He is not an A-1 student. I am always very frank, Mr. Lew, you know that, so I will tell you: my son is not top notch. However. He tries hard. Very hard. That's why he is applying to the school where your son teaches."

"Where my son teaches? Ah." My father sits a little taller.

"You understand —"

"Of course. Naturally."

"All these years, working here — we should really be doing something, hm? You should be in government, Mr. Lew. And me? I should be teaching. However," Mrs. Ma smiles at my father, "What do we do?"

"We go and make money," he snorts.

Mrs. Ma laughs. She and my father appreciate each

other. They know the price of things, what the future costs, what each has paid.

"You're lucky," Mrs. Ma tells my father, "Your children are doing so well."

"My children? Oh, they're just working. Workingworking."

"Yes, but *working*."

Mrs. Ma reminds my father he can take it a little easy now, he is already clipping coupons, so to speak, while she has a ways to go; her children are still in school.

"How about a scholarship?" she says. "Do you think we can get a scholarship? My son, his grades are not the best, you know."

"Not the best? Hm. Well. Maybe you should try anyway. You don't try, you don't get it. You better try."

"You think so?"

"Sure. Go ahead. I would."

"You would? Oh, Mr. Lew, that's just what I was thinking, myself, but what do I know? I'm so glad to hear you say this. You agree with me!"

Mrs. Ma turns her full smile on my father. For a moment he wonders, what has he agreed to? In a day full of wrong turns and missed connections, is he finally connecting? Is this possible? With Mrs. Ma? She once told him, "Mr.Lew, we're the same, you know, you and me. We look things straight in the face and we say what we think. We don't care, do we?"

"More tea?" she freshens his cup. She's holding her smile. Her eyes look pinched. She is waiting for him to say something.

My father rushes in. "I'll talk to him," he promises. "Yes, yes. I'll tell my son. Of course. He can take care of everything."

Back in his car, he puts on his baseball hat and hangs his chin over the steering wheel. He drives the Beltway back. It's late, almost supper time, though the summer light still holds. He wonders if my mother has set the police on him. He keeps checking his rear-view mirror. He should have called her, but what could he say? I spent the afternoon with Mrs. Ma? And it went from one thing to the next?

His car eats up the miles. He's going no faster than before, but because he's returning home instead of leaving, the road flows by easier. All the signs that tricked him on the way out, now wave him on: Landover, Suitland, Oxon Hill. Big green messages ticking by. My father gives them his full attention.

One says, your wife is looking out the window. Two miles.

The next says, Wilson Bridge.

The next, Slow, she is talking to your son.

The next, Alexandria. She is going to yell at you.

Five miles, two, one, he exits the Beltway and barely stops at a stop sign. He's hungry and tired. His bladder is urging him on. He cuts off someone who honks at him. Tough. Maybe he doesn't drive so good. Maybe he can't yell at other drivers like they yell at him, his English not good enough, maybe, maybe. Who cares. Maybe he doesn't know north, south, east west, where is he going on what road. Maybe. But he's come this far, hasn't he? From a house looking over a paddy field to this, a nice family place. Good value, like his real estate agent says, solid brick, colonial. Sometimes it surprises him to think, at the end of the road, this is home, this and not the old mud brick house he grew up in.

He used to go to market with his father, and on the way home they always stopped at the top of the last hill to look for their house, take a leak. Who would think he would leave one morning, and upon his return he would see from that hill the whole village burning. Was it the bandits? Or the soldiers? He left then, and kept going and going until he got to here. Three bedrooms with wood paneling. Not so shabby. Even so, if this is here and this is home, then the other, the mud brick, the mother making his shoes, the father telling him that everything, everything will be his, where has that gone now?

He turns onto his street, feeling the weight of time and the distance he has driven to get here. The sight of Mrs. Macomber, however, revives him. She is walking her dog toward his tree.

He toots his horn and the dog jumps, dragging Mrs. Macomber back to her own yard.

"Hello, Pete," he cuts a sharp left. Zooms into his drive.

Maybe he doesn't always know his way around, maybe he will know only one way around at one time, who can say. One thing sure though, he never forgets where he wants to go and he gets there somehow, doesn't he?

He goes into the house and my mother comes running. "Where have you been?"

"Where do you think?" he hands her a white bucket. This is what he has gone all the way around the Beltway to get.

"Tofu?" she screams.

"Of course. You cannot get it fresh here. You know that. Don't you like it fresh?"

He cooks up what he has brought himself — my mother won't touch it — and the tofu turns out to be really so tender, like custard, like pudding, it seems entirely plausible that someone would circle the Beltway, the globe, even, from rice field to quarter-acre lot, and along the way, there to here, defy the rules of the road, the rules of language, of expectation, to get just what he wants.

My father bends over his plate. He rests an arm on the table and only his wrist moves, dishing up the tofu.

*Arrh, Arrh, gokgokgok*
*Ah Fong, Ah Fong, arrrharrrh*
*Gokgokgok . . . gukgukguk . . .*

ALL DAY, IT GOES like this: the girls at the take-out counter slamming out the dim sum, while the kitchen sends — through the intercom — its stream of consciousness.

*Arrharrharrh!*

A little white speaker, embedded in a white wall, generates gym-sized echoes. All day, it emits ear-numbing volumes. The speaker cannot communicate, but picks up speech and recycles it to garbage. For this reason, its distortions are more fabulous than the dumplings over which it rules. Those who know go to that dim sum counter to connect, not only with the familiar comforts of cake and dumpling, but with their remembered decibels.

## BELOW THE LINE

IT BOTHERS ME. When I say my life is spinning round and round, people think I'm speaking metaphorically — especially in my business, where we do things over and over, so we can make what's not real more real. So we can eat pie, the same bite, five times; replay the sweating climax ten times; live life larger than life. Life as a huge, symphonically enhanced landscape; life as an excruciatingly meaningless close-up.

Cars crash, lips meet; in my business we're big on metaphors. We get paid by the metaphor. We dress the set, trim the lights, cheat the angles, doctor the story, auteur the film. Whatever needs doing, we do it, and the more the metaphors pile on, the higher we rise, maybe even to top billing on a marquee. Once there, who knows, the only thing left to do is to become an icon. A Marilyn. A Jimmy. Not anything smelling of incense, but an American icon. The best. We still make the best. Our icons are the Cadillacs of metaphors. Big, eye-catching, they ride into the little screens of our minds and take over. Great chrome. Great curves.

In my business, we're always getting carried away with the big idea. It's our job, to work the metaphor, make the movie. It's always been this way. But, as far as I can recall — it's been a few years now that I've worked on the front lines of the industry; I can't speak for the front office, but from the front lines — I sincerely cannot ever recall hearing the word itself used the way it is today, like a reflex. Like something you do as easily as eating, or drinking, or falling into bed with someone you like. So it is with metaphor: you have to get comfortable with it, relaxed about dropping the word socially. It's become one of those things you talk about when you lead the kind of life we do in the business, fully involved and bi-coastal.

There was the time I met a grip — he's the guy who builds special rigs and mounts for lights and camera — and I asked, "How come the camera's shaking like that?"

We had just filmed a scene from a vampire's point of view. The grip wore black T-shirts and white T-shirts on alternating days. I liked him, we were all working for nothing, and he said, "It's a metaphor."

I said, "Yeah?"

He said, "C'mere." He took me by the hand and led me to a rig he and the cameraman had devised to shake their metaphor. "Take a look." He turned it on for me.

I put my eye to the camera. I now had vampire vision; everything vibrated. "That's the concept?" I said.

"That's it." The grip noted my expression. "Girl, where you been? Vampires need blood like winos need wine. They don't get it, they get the shakes."

He laughed and mussed my hair. I went out with him later. Not for a drink that time, but for an ice cream cone. Soon after, our vampire movie collapsed. As it was meant to. Its director had settled for cheap shots because he couldn't afford the real, dollar-actuated digital effects. From the beginning, he had been hiding from his investors, a handful of credit card companies and two older sisters who thought they were paying for business school. So, maybe it has been money, or the lack of money, that accounts for the proliferation of metaphor. When nothing else is available, we have to fall back on it, don't we.

When I say my life is spinning round and round, I'm not making anything up, I'm saying it for real. The other day I went to Chinatown to do my shopping. I never thought I would — go back, that is — when I didn't have to. Kind of like those old Cantonese ladies who no longer live in Chinatown but still return, Saturday after Saturday. They're genetically programmed to do this, the old ladies. They can't leave behind the doorway where they get the best gossip, the spot in front of the dim sum palace where they get the best view — who's having the wedding inside and how big. They can't miss the favorite corner where a cousin has opened a shop, the bakery where an old friend will slip a sweet bun across the counter, the beauty shop where old friends line up against a wall and, sitting in their plastic chairs, pull down the matching plastic dryers that will lock everything in place, every curl, every speck of dye, every memory. It's with these dryers that the old ladies replicate time. Week after week they submit, and emerge looking like the perfect copy of themselves some thirty years ago. Their hair always comes out pouffed to the same exacting stiffness.

They've moved on to good houses, fresh air, these ladies getting their hair done. There are others, though, who've remained behind in the brick buildings, the old rooms. They're the grannies who cut their own hair and sport the Chinatown look, the one built around the vest. This vest comes in muted colors, brown or gray, cloth or knit. Floral designs are popular, too. Imported from the old village in Canton, the vest looks about the same hanging on a clothesline as it does on an old lady. All the vests worn now are descended from the very first vest made by taking the suitcoat of an American Baptist missionary and chopping its sleeves off. Perhaps because of this history, the Chinatown vests are totally indifferent to whatever body might be occupying them.

The old ladies who wear the vests crowd the sidewalks on a good day. They hunt for bargains, buy pork, squeeze the fruit. But this is only what it looks like they're doing. In truth, they're up to something else: they assault the bus when it arrives, they attack a fresh crate of fish when it's unloaded. They throw bags of plums at grocery clerks, cut in front to pick over green beans, hold up a line to dig for pennies. They show up Saturday after Saturday, not for shopping, really, but for troop maneuvers. To test the rest of us. To keep themselves in shape. They push and shove because that's what they do: they come to renew their claim to this place, to the fish and jade and duck and noodles and spit and grease — to all of it.

The old ladies are tough. Too tough for me. Normally, I wouldn't think of going to Chinatown on a Saturday when they're out in force, but the other day I had to. I had to buy sugar snap peas. Green pods of exquisite crunchiness, these peas fill the ears with the sound of masticating — is their sound as much a part of their taste as their taste?

I had to have them. Basil, too, the kind the Hmong grow, smaller-leaved than Italian basil, green with a touch of purple, the stem dark, almost woody. I set out and shopped in what became an ever-enlarging circle, from my neighborhood to another neighborhood, to new Chinatown and finally on to original Chinatown.

In original Chinatown, I looked for the basil and the peas. I saw a man coming at me, a man I'd seen before when his eyes were so hot and yellow they parted crowds. Now, they were merely blank. I passed the man and bought what I'd come for, but then I couldn't seem to leave.

Maybe it was the Saturday crush. The old ladies. They were confusing me with their activity. One group had already closed in on a man passing out tins of cookies. Another was about to arrive with the change of traffic lights down the street. For a moment, as I stood waiting for my own light to change, all the old ladies in Chinatown seemed to be bearing down on me. A few had stenciled brows, freshly dyed hair. Others wore the trademark vests with pants that stopped short of their shoes. All carried bags, limp ones hanging from one finger, or big plastic things weighted with chicken and shrimp and cabbage and melon and bean sauce and hot sauce. I wondered whether to get out of their way, or to let the old ladies and their tide of single-mindedness drive me forward. Lately, so many things seemed to be slowing me down.

I decided to go for hot sauce. I crossed the street, then circled back, this time for mussels, I don't know why, maybe because an old lady pushed me into them. A great bin of green-lipped mussels almost too pretty to eat. They would make a stylish arrangement around the rim of a platter, pasta mounded in the center, mussels claiming the edge, so inviting, the green-lipped shells yawning open. I bought a bag and returned to my car. On the way, I tangled with a crowd rocking a pickup truck. People pushed and threw their hands up in the air. I couldn't get around. Finally, I threw my hand up, too. After some jostling, it came back to me, my hand, that is, and I saw I'd won a bag of loquats. Pale orange fruit still clinging to their branch.

I worked my way out of Chinatown and went to see my brother. He had an office just down the hill. It was Saturday, but I knew I'd find him behind his desk or at his telescope enjoying the view. In one direction, he had the gorgeous bay. In the other, a Penthouse pet.

My brother works nearly every weekend. He is older. He makes a lot of money. He's been touted as the lawyer for the Pacific Rim. His favorite activity is matchmaking: putting the right money together with the right people. He is always trying to matchmake for me, too. He doesn't understand how I can live on my median income. He gives me his used car, his TV, and most recently his bed — he wants something wrought-iron and contemporary. My brother is always handing me things. I do what I can for him.

That Saturday, after buying so much in Chinatown, I went to his office and unloaded my bags on his conference table. "You want some of this?" I said.

I caught my brother on the phone, not the telescope. Too bad. He threw a newspaper at me.

"Okay, okay." I spread the paper out and put my bags on top of the paper.

When he got off the phone, my brother stayed behind his desk and just looked at me. Looked at all the things I'd brought. He shook his head. "Not again," he said.

I didn't want to think about it, but I guess he was right. I do have a habit and it still gets to me now and then. But it's only when I see food — food, fresh and plentiful, food in its raw state, that's when I can't resist. I buy and buy and buy until I'm out of money or too loaded down with bags to move. I really do shop until I drop, but unlike other people who defend their excess by claiming they've really found a bargain and it's going to last forever, I never bother with such excuses. I have no compunction: I buy just to buy. I buy only what is wonderful and at its peak the instant I see it. I buy the beautifully muscled salmon. The perfectly red pepper. I don't think of what will happen once the salmon is lifted from its bed of ice. Or the pepper removed from the ray of sun that gives it its gloss. I don't think far enough ahead. That's what my brother says. Or perhaps I do. Which is why I must have what I see when I see it. Otherwise, later, it won't be beautiful any more, will it.

My brother has told me, and so has my doctor, to eat well before going out and to avoid certain places like farmers' markets or Chinatown, where the synergy of fresh produce and determined shoppers pushes me over the edge. My adrenalin goes into overdrive, and the aggression my doctor says I could better apply to my life in general gets wasted lunging for a fish. Or a crab. Or a bag of scallops.

It's hard. I'm told to take time out, breathe deep. I'm allowed to carry only twenty dollars in cash, though this doesn't work as a real restraint, since it's easy enough to break down and go to an automatic teller machine whenever I'm in the grip of one of my elevated shopping states. The best solution, really, has been to stick to supermarkets. There's nothing there to excite the appetite.

"Don't say anything," I told my brother now. "It's too late." I laid out my purchases and pulled plastic bag from plastic bag. "What do you want? You still seeing Lily?"

He pursed his mouth.

"She like mussels?"

"Doesn't cook 'em."

"You cook 'em. How about scallops?"

"Yeah."

"Shrimp?"

"Yeah."

"Eggplant?"

"Nah — you busy?"

My brother suddenly switched the subject on me. He had a way of doing this. Only a few weeks ago, when I'd gone to pick up the bed he was giving me, he caught me with the same question, and, like now, he asked it when my back was turned.

On that occasion, I replied, "Busy? Not really." I soon found myself helping him cook a dinner for six. He needed to impress a fashionable young couple who had just come into a lot of money. For that dinner, I created a de-boned orange-scented duck stuffed with wild rice and mushrooms. I stir-fried sugar snap peas, which have become kind of a signature dish for me.

"A touch of oil, no salt," I told the guests. "The peas don't need it, they're sweet. But if you must, add it like you do vermouth to a martini Pass your hand over like that, barely, and that's all the salt you need."

I made salad with greens from my garden and strawberry ice with a machine my brother had given me. I sent him out for flowers and arranged a big, warm display. My brother only likes hard surfaces, he has steel shelves and glass tables. He likes things streamlined, polished. He is surgical in the way he goes after what he wants. Not like me. As I said, I go in circles, but my brother, he cuts through. I think because we grew up where there were no Chinatowns or old ladies to patrol the streets for us, my brother learned early on that he had to do it for himself. He had to cut through whatever stood in his way, and he did, with a nicely honed ruthlessness. I once heard him tell an old friend, "Sure, you can go ahead and tell me how much you need, but how're you planning to pay me back?"

My brother cut a path from our small town to the big world beyond. Naturally, I followed. After all, if he had already blazed a way out, why should I look for another? My brother made his way to Chinatown, the lucrative edge of it, and some years later, I followed. I lived in a building he owned up the hill, and, until I moved, I used to shop in Chinatown every week with the patrols of old ladies in their blue and gray vests.

For my brother's dinner, I may have overdone it, but I took the flowers he bought and deployed them throughout his place. A bloom of color at every turn to distract from his hard edges.

My brother served the wine. Made the coffee. Afterward, he said he was proud of me, his dinner was such a success. He called our mother to tell her. She likes hearing things like this. She in turn called me. She called so early one morning, she frightened me out of my sleep.

"Ma," I said, "Are you all right? "

"May, May," she replied, "Gary tell me you cook him a million-dollar dinner.

"Ma —"

"It's true."

"Ma —"

"Those people hire him, he make millions."

"I'm going back to sleep."

"May, you listen, May — May? You two stick together, hah? You do this, you can do anything. Anything. You know that?"

My mother is a believer. She believes in God. She believes in Jesus. She believes in the Bible. She also believes that when people are related, blood makes them stick together, blood sees them through.

I think my mother has her point, but for my brother and me there is something else at work. What holds us together, different as we are, is that we have survived the same metaphors. We grew up where people called us commies, pinkos, japs, and every now and then they got it right: chink.

It was beautiful, this place without a Chinatown that we called home. In winter, the snow came down in flurries of white and everything looked like those paperweights that were made to be shaken and shaken, until their worlds under glass came alive to their own neatly contrived magic.

My brother and I loved where we grew up, but we also learned how things from outside could come along and shake us, too. We learned what it was like to be turned into someone else's metaphor. To be someone else's pinko, someone else's jap, someone else's chinaman. To get caught on the wrong side of a word. We learned that metaphor wasn't high concept. On the contrary, metaphor packed a punch. My brother fought his way through his and eventually created his own vision of what he was, an operator on Pacific waters. I, on the other hand, threw these words back at people who threw them at me. I was pretty good at this because I talked fast and, better yet, when my words backfired, I ran even faster. Eventually though, I had to figure out for myself what other words could replace the ones I threw away.

In my brother's office, I kept pulling items from my plastic bags. They seemed bottomless now and filled with things I had to unwrap to recall what they were. Frozen dumplings? Two kinds of noodles? Did I buy these?

My brother lost his patience, "Put that away, will you?"

He got up and stuffed things back into my bags. Only the things he really didn't want, though, I noticed. The eggplant, the chili — those were going with me.

My brother doesn't lose sight of what he's after. "You busy?" he returned to what had been on his mind. "I want you to come next Tuesday." He handed me my bags.

"Here?" I said.

"Ten o'clock."

"Okay, okay."

My brother lives in a world of precision and movement. Time goes forward for him, it piles up in dollars. I thought, maybe for once I should do it like he does.

It's my job to put a reel of tape on a tape recorder and watch life go round and round. Not my life, necessarily, but other people's lives. People who are telling me things. I watch thirty minutes go by, then I put on another reel of tape and I do this for another thirty minutes, maybe less. I do it until the director says cut.

On my job, I record people talking and singing, whatever I've been hired to do. I tape the sounds my subjects make; they're not always human. I've recorded dogs and cats and birds and large mammals. On occasion, snakes and insects, too. While most of my subjects prove to be human, the sounds they make are not always species-specific.

I remember the famous public figure who came across as a veritable frog speaking from the bottom of a well. The man had a reputation as a prince, a prince of diplomacy, a prince to the fabulously well-connected. While I was recording him, though, he remained, quite adamantly, a frog, pop-eyed and unreactive. His voice rose in muddy emissions from his belly. Then, there was the woman who could not stop chirping. We wasted an hour of tape trying to lure her into a revealing anecdote, but, cricket that she was, the woman never once let up or changed her cheery tune.

I told my brother about the cricket and the frog and the many others I had recorded. My brother is a good brother. He has taken the time to see the films I've worked on, he always asks what I'm doing, but I'm not sure he really understands what I tell him. He knows I make a steady wage; I support myself. Still, he doesn't like what I do, and I'm afraid he talks to my doctor about this.

My brother has seen film budgets — more and more in recent years. People have taken to calling him with the flimsiest of introductions. They're trolling for Asians with deep pockets, but my brother isn't star-struck. He looks to the bottom line. He knows only the select few get a percentage of the gross, while no one ever sees a percentage of the net. He also knows that the ones who get the real money and big credits are, as we say in the industry, the ones above the line — the stars, the directors, the writers — while the ones below the line are the household staff. We light and record and dress and feed and clean up. My brother has a keen nose for who is a real player and who is not. He wants me to be a player. But what I like is cooking. I'm not afraid to say this, "I like to cook." I stand up to my brother, but does he listen? I have to tell my doctor instead.

"Doctor," I say, "I have to make steamed fish with scallions, broiled salmon with light teriyaki, ribs with my own tangy hot pineapple barbecue sauce, range chicken with rosemary, pork butt slow-cooked in soy the way my father does it. I am not a vegetarian, doctor, I like fat and I like meat and I like cooking them both together. I cook them well. As for vegetables, I appreciate them, too. I let them be. This is the only way to get into their groove, the snap of snap peas, the crunch of carrots, the munch of lettuce. The sound of chewing fiber induces a meditation, just look at cows. I believe in the curative powers of green leaves.

"I also make rice and pasta and fresh bread."

"Are you happy, then?" my doctor says.

"Happy?" I'm annoyed by her intrusion. "Busy. When I cook, I'm busy."

Because my brother does not like what I do, because he wants me to be making at least ten thousand more a year, he has been pushing me to start my own business. I think this is why he set me up with the appointments in his office. He would have preferred something more ambitious, but my doctor told him to go slow. She saw me every week and did nothing but sit with her knees addressing mine. Nonetheless, she reported to my brother that I was going to need many more sessions with her. I had what she called serious boundary issues to explore; she did not want me taking on additional complications. So, to help me out, my brother had to start with a small project, something requested by a rich and dying client of his.

At the appointed hour, I was ready. My brother brought in his client. He helped the old man to a chair I had placed by a window. "Ah," the old man looked around, "This is it?" He fell into his chair.

My brother's secretary brought in a cup of tea.

The old man looked at me and the video camera I had set on a tripod facing him.

"This is May," my brother introduced me.

"May I?" I approached the old man with a microphone in my hand.

"May?" he said.

"Yes," I bent over him. "May I?"

"May?" he cranked up his hearing aid.

"Yes," I almost shouted, "I am May and I want to put this on you. Hold still." I clipped my microphone to the old man's tie.

He smiled, "How old are you?"

My brother intervened, "When she says go ahead, you go ahead. Now, you remember what you want to say?"

"Yah."

"You ready?"

"Yah."

"May?"

"Go ahead."

"Mr. Ho?"

"Hah?"

"Ho Siansheng! "

"Ah, ah."

"Talk to her!" My brother shouted at the old man and left the room to take a phone call. He kept an eye on us through an open door.

The old man spread his legs, planted his hands on his knees. "I am here," he looked into the camera, "because I want you to see I am of sound mind. And my body? I still have what's left."

The old man struck his chest. "No one. No one is putting words in my mouth. I'm putting them in myself. She can tell you."

He paused, waved a hand at me. "Come here."

I hesitated. Looked to my brother.

"You need help?" he glanced over and went right on talking into his phone.

The old man hit the arm of his chair. "Come here! Don't turn off —"

I went to him.

"Look," he pulled me down to face the camera, "This is May. Kitty, you never looked so good. May is sound mind, and her body? Look. See? Her brother is my lawyer, he can tell you, this May, she's good shape."

The old man squeezed my arm and pushed me back to my camera.

"May here's pretty enough, I'm doing everything she tells me. I'm going on her camera — how do you say — live. Yah. Hahaha. Live. Before you forget, I'm telling you. All this years, I give you everything, condo, car, fur coat, not the cheap kind from Korea, but real sable. I save you from Cho-Cho's. Give you more money than you ever see from any customer. And what do you do? You treat me like I'm gone already.

"Well, surprise. I'm here," the old man raised a hand. "I'm never go away. I'm here forever. For you. On this TV. And you are going to listen, yah, to me. You are going to listen because if you don't, you don't get nothing.

"Number one. You promise take care me, you never take care me. I am so sick.

"Number two. You promise never go back to Cho-Cho, that kind of business. But I know, you go out. Every night.

"Number three. You have new boyfriend. Let him buy you a house.

"Number four. You are not my wife. My wife is my wife. My wife is in China. She knows, if she wants what I have, she better come now. She's coming.

"Number five. Now, I am at the end, I give you one thousand. You want more? You already took it. Hahaha.

"I am Ho Cheng-hsin."

The old man finished with his chin up and his mouth pulled down.

This was the first video will my brother arranged for me to tape. The others didn't get any better. Several were straightforward lists of gifts and bequests. Why people wanted to do their wills on video, I never quite understood. I guess there was the power that video gave them to deny death, to talk on and on without anyone talking back. Best of all, it gave people a chance to excite their loved ones from beyond the grave in a way that they had not been able to excite them in life. All my brother's clients had spent time watching TV with their families. They could imagine what would happen when they themselves became the show. They knew who would sit where for what they called the viewing. Who would flinch or cry or go red-eyed with rage. Knowing this, they made sure to set it up with my brother in such a way that this person had to listen to his message and that one to hers, before anyone could get a dime. Just as TV froze people in front of its flicker, so these wills were made to freeze angry families before their droning grandfathers. For some of the old men, this was probably the closest they ever came to getting the old kowtow.

A few people, however, used their videos to say from the far reach of death what they had not been able to say in the intimacy of life. Thus, one man who had arrived here a penniless refugee, but was preparing to leave this world a wealthy man, said:

"You are my son. I am my father's son. My father is his father's son and his father is his father's father's son. We go back five generations. More, I cannot say for sure. However, I know this: we cannot stop now.

"Though you do not listen to me any more, I am still your father and you are still my son. This you can never change, even you want to. You are my son. And because of this you are a boy. This is how you were born. This is how you will die: a boy, not a girl. You can never be a girl, even you beg for it. Do you know why? Because you were born a boy. A boy is born a boy so he does not have to be a girl. A girl is born a girl so she cannot be a boy. This is the way of the world. There is no other. This is how we come together and make one generation after another: because you are the boy and someone else is the girl.

"Please. I beg you, be reasonable. Marry and have sons. I am your father."

This man would not look at me after his taping; he was too embarrassed. But he reminded me of something; he brought me back to what it was I was really doing: I put tape to tape recorder, not to hear people reciting their wills, not to record the petty balance sheet of a life, nor its vindictive economies, "You want to be poor, be poor; you don't get one dollar more, not from me." No, I didn't roll tape even to witness the tender moments, "I give you my watch, and you my gold ring." I rolled only to listen to the sounds people made as they struggled with their lives, the way this father was doing. The burping, coughing, hemming, hawing, breaking wind, breaking thought, sniffling, crying, choking, gulping, and yes, even the pissing in the pants of an old man stumped for a thought.

I listened for these sounds, whatever they were, however they came to me, and over the years I heard so much that I became an accomplice of sorts. I became, not the hired gun, nor the hired hand, but the hired ear. Yes, with my tape recorder hanging heavy from my shoulder, my microphone formidable from its pole, I transformed myself into the very appendage that everyone wanted: I became the willing ear. Indeed, I applied my ear to whatever was asked of me. I dressed in skinny black and kept my face white. People called from both coasts to ask for my services. If I wanted, I could have earned more for my work, much more, even after deductions to my union. Yet all I did, just to keep things fresh, was to change my hair from black to bleached, and back to black again, once every three months.

The director would say. "Roll sound." I would roll, and the subject would start up, make a noise in the belly, the throat, then these terrible stories would come out.

They reeled onto my tape. I didn't stop them, I couldn't. I was being paid to keep everything rolling, stories of incest, rape, murder, beatings. I had to empty my face, make it nothing. And like the black-clad figure who runs from stage left, lays out the table, the tea cup, and disappears stage right, I, too, became a servant of ceremony, and in this way, I like to think I rose above my hourly wage, my overtime: I learned to preside over the cruelest of scenes but never let emotion shake my hand, weaken my grip. I held my microphone steady, and whatever came, I refused to let it modulate beyond my control. I kept it all within the bounds of quarter-inch tape. Fear and joy, I rolled right through.

I heard a woman say, "Then my father came into my room and laid down on top of me." I heard the tape hiss, the woman cry. Such terrors I heard, I took my ears off, in my sleep, and offered them up for absolution.

The father who begged his son to listen to reason left quickly after his taping. I remembered only later where I had seen him before. He had a big voice and swollen hands flushed a deep red. The voice he used to yell at his customers. The hands he never looked at, but they cut ducks all day long. I remember now he had the shop next to the fire station. His ducks were always sold out by three in the afternoon.

My brother left on a business trip. While he was gone, I ignored the calls I got from his secretary requesting more dates for more videos. I went back to producers I had worked with before and landed a couple of film jobs. By the time my brother returned, I was able to tell him, in all honesty, "I'm busy. I'm booked." If I hadn't, I think I might have had to tape not only more wills but product catalogues and promotional videos for several companies owned by friends of his.

As luck would have it, I worked hard for a couple of months, then I ran into a string of problems with my recordings. One day an interview was fed out of sync to a video deck. I corrected this, but on the very next interview, the subject, a tall thin man, came in with a stutter so bad, the effect was as if I were listening, again, to something out of sync. I had to take my headphones off to make sure the man was indeed speaking a beat behind himself.

Soon after this, strange contaminations started appearing spontaneously and totally randomly on my recordings. They appeared as faint but audible penumbras of electronic noise around certain peak levels of sound. I tried changing tapes, recording at a lower level, cleaning the heads on my recorder, testing my microphones. Still, the odd and totally irregular blossomings of electronic noise would appear.

I took my tape recorder to a sound genius. He lived in a deep well of silence and padded about in stocking feet. His dog would yap and then he would surface, blinking and making the mildest of statements, "Weell, I'll take a look." He took my recorder and, a week later, reported he hadn't been able to duplicate my problem, but he had checked out everything and everything was all right; I had one of the quietest machines he had ever worked on. Later, I heard other people claim he had told them the same thing, but I didn't mind. In a time of uncertainty, what I wanted most was to believe that if one man said it was so, it was so.

Whatever the sound genius did or did not do, the contaminations went away. At this time I also stopped recording for a while. This helped the problem, too. I got involved with my friend April's brother. April said, "I think you'll get along, you're both weird." How weird, I don't think she knew. Nor did I.

Her brother was beautiful. He had skinny hips and coarse hair. He wore his pants slung low, his hair long. We went at it for several weeks. Then we took time out for other things. He showed me the tattoos he custom-designed. Japanese waves, mythical creatures, totemic symbols from Tibet, Japan, Korea. He said he was orphaned because he was neither this nor that, neither Japanese nor Korean, neither American nor immigrant. His Korean mother had brought him and April here when they were starting school. I said, "That's like us, Gary and me. We came when we were little, too."

Unlike my brother, however, Steve hadn't grown up to chase big bucks. I could talk to him about things I never bothered bringing up with Gary. Things like my collection of tape recordings. In my place, I had a wall of burps and rumbles and gaffes and weird laughs, next to peacocks screaming, buffalo snuffing, horses thundering, next to yelps and whoops and whistles, next to — and this was my favorite — next to two shelves' worth of great and singular voices. In this category, there were the mumblers, the squeakers, the basso profoundos and the bella-cantoed sopranos. There were the liars, the lied-to, the fatuous, the sincere and, tops on my list, the man who answered every question he was asked by squawking, "Desalinization plants. Yawp. That's what we need."

I spent a couple evenings unreeling these treasures to Steve. He got into the weirdness of them right away and started sampling my recordings for himself. The pig roast with the unholy screams of pigs falling to the slaughter, the shrill cries of children running up to wash their hands in the blood. Steve was so taken with what I had, I thought, maybe I'll try something else out on him. I'll tell him about the video I'm planning to make.

"It's about this old lady I've been following around," I said. "She's somebody I always see when I buy pork in Chinatown. She's there every Saturday. She's got the permed hair and creamy skin. I want to put her in my video. I want her to do what she does. No acting, just what she does. Go to the beauty shop, get her hair blasted. Buy pork, veggies, then go to the Italian deli. And there she stands in front of Joe, he owns the place, and he's got the stomach and the apron and he says, 'You want the salami?'

"'Eh-eh,' the old lady says. I'll call her Mrs. Chan.

"'Ham?'

"'Eh.'

"'Bologna?'

"'Eh.'

"'Olives?'

"'Hah?'

"'Olives? Here, olives,' Joe gives Mrs. Chan an olive. 'You want?'

"'Nh.'

"'No?'

"'Nh-nh,' shakes her head.

"'Turkey?'

"'Eh.'

"'Tomatoes?'

"'Nh.'

"'Bread?'

"'Eh.'

"'What kind? This?'

"'Eh.'

"'Or this?'

"'Eh-eh.'

"'This?'

"'Eh.'

"And so on — Joe and Mrs. Chan. Eh-eh, nh-nh, eh-eh. Two good people grunting and nodding at each other. A little finger pointing here and there, too. That's all, that's all you'd need. What do you think?"

I turned to look at Steve. He'd fallen asleep. His hair lay thick over the side of his face. I lifted it and saw the angle of his jaw. His ear. He was so perfect. I thought, "Now I've done it, I've gone on too long. I've talked him to sleep."

I bent and licked his ear. I ran my tongue around the thin gold hoop he had in it. I nuzzled. He moved. I nuzzled some more. He woke up and smiled. He had the broadest forehead, the droopiest eyes. He stretched like a cat and turned his face into the pillow. His left ear presented itself to me now. I saw its tight whorls, its neat curve down to a thick lobe. I bent my face to it, and when I had that fleshy part in my mouth, it came to me then, "So this is what it's like to talk someone's ear off." I pressed my teeth together suddenly; I surprised myself. I brought the taste of blood to my tongue.

Not long after, April called and said, "What's going on? What're you doing to my brother?"

My brother called and said, "Did you have to injure the guy? Is he going to sue?"

I said, "No, Steve's okay. I put some ointment on his ear. And I'm buying him a new earring."

"A new earring?"

"Yeah, for the one I bent out of shape."

"Jesus." My brother hung up on me.

Next, my mother called. "She said, Gary say you not feeling so good. You okay?"

"I'm okay."

"You don't have a cold? Sound like you have a cold. Your nose."

"It's nothing."

"I can hear it."

"It's allergies, Ma, allergies."

"Allergies. Oh. I thought you over that already. I thought it's something else." My mother paused. She was good at milking things out of me. I let her wheeze for a while, then I gave in.

"Okay. All right. What did Gary tell you?" I said.

"Gary?"

"Yeah. Gary."

"Gary, yeah. He say — you don't get mad at him?"

"No, I don't get mad at him."

"He's your brother. He loves you."

"Yeah, I know. What did he say?"

"He say, she's sick puppy."

"He said that?"

"Yeah. One sick one."

"My brother said that?"

"Yeah. What's that mean, May? What's that mean?"

I didn't have a clue. For days I waited by my phone. I waited for an answer, I waited for the mail. All that came to me were messages from my doctor, "Call me," and from my producer, "We start Monday, six o'clock."

Then, what I'd been looking for arrived. It came as a card, with a picture of a vampire drawn on one side. On the other, there was an ear, and over the ear, Steve had printed, "My turn next. Watch yourself!"

Was this friendly or was this hostile? I couldn't decide. At the bottom of the card, he had added, "No hard feelings." The word "hard" was underlined and trailed off into a scribbled, "Ha, ha, ha."

I went to see my doctor. "Doctor," I said, "what does this mean?"

Perhaps I asked too shrilly. My doctor responded, "I want to put you on medication."

I said, "But he's all right. He didn't even need to go to the hospital."

She said, "That's not the issue."

I said, "Have you been trying out another one of my recipes?"

My doctor has been getting fatter and fatter right before my eyes. She fills up with all the stuff she hears from Gary, though she denies it. I'm sure she's talked to him about Steve. My doctor has gained twenty pounds since I've been seeing her. She's ingested every word I've said, the conversations I've recorded, the meals I've cooked, the new things I've introduced her to.

"Did you ever find that hairy one?" I said.

"What?"

I'd startled her.

"Rambutan. The red one with hair all over. Not firm but rubbery."

"No, I don't believe . . . no, I've never seen one, not like that, exactly." My doctor always has to sound like she knows what she's talking about.

"It's a fruit, for godssake," I snapped at her.

She looked sharp.

"Did you ever find it?" I said finally.

"No. Did you?"

"Of course. That's why I'm telling you."

I sat in my chair and looked at my doctor and she looked at me. I wondered why I bothered telling this woman things she didn't get. I wondered what else I was going to have to dig up to feed her. I wondered, how had I fallen into this room with its pale walls, its gray carpet, its soft, soft light?

I drove straight through, the night black before me, the radio quiet. Space-pod rest stations glowed in the distance, orbited by. The road offered no obstacle. Only my mind racketed through.

I arrived at dawn, exhausted. Red-eyed. My mother ran into the kitchen as I banged in. She screamed.

"It's me," I said. "Just me."

"Watch the door," she scolded. "You break it, you pay for it. "

"I didn't do anything. Relax."

I dropped into a chair by the kitchen table. "Where's Dad?" I asked.

My mother went to the stairs and yelled. "It's May. Go back to sleep." She returned to the kitchen. "What you doing here?"

I looked at her. She was wearing one of those Chinatown vests. Her hair had gone dry and gray. She used to knit the vests all through my childhood but I never understood why they had to come out so shapeless. Why they always gave up at the arms. I never appreciated the vests my mother knit until I grew up and went to Chinatown. And then I learned, only women of a certain age wear these vests. They are the ones you cannot cross, the ones you do not pick a fight with, the ones you dare not cheat. These vests, I learned, come vested with authority. "That's a new one, isn't it?" I pointed to my mother's.

She repeated her question, "What you doing here?" But I couldn't tell her. Not the truth. I couldn't say, "I talked my boyfriend's ear off. It got messy, Ma. That blanket you gave me? It got little drops of blood on it. And Gary and my doctor? They're mad at me, Ma, they're really mad at me."

I couldn't say this, what had happened, so I said instead, "I'm coming home for a while, Ma. Is that all right?"

I laid in my old room and squeezed my eyes shut. I listened for the sounds to come back. The tree scratching the side of the house, the dog down the road. In the morning there were the birds and two deep woofwoofs as Mr.Corrigan walked his shepherd by. My bed still creaked when I got out of it.

My father took me to his restaurant. There wasn't much to do. I scribbled orders or sat with him by the cash register. The new man cooked in the kitchen and his sister — he wasn't married yet — his sister waited on the tables. This was how we had started here. My father cooking in the kitchen, my mother working out front. We had been imported by the previous owner to work his restaurant. My father had bought that man out, and now, he, in turn, had just had the pleasure of importing his own man from his own village to succeed him.

He said, "Last time I go home, gee, fifty people want to talk to me. Everyone all at once. So loud." My father wrinkled his face, "I not used to it any more. They all want to come over. This good business, you know." He looked at me. "You sure you don't want it?"

I looked at him.

He sighed. "Gary don't need it, but you. I don't know. You run all over. What's so good about that?"

"It's my job, dad, I have to travel."

"Travel? Travel, travel. Why don't you go to school? Law school I pay."

"We already have a lawyer in the family."

"That's bad?"

"Mmm."

"You get a degree, Gary give you a job. You don't even have to ask."

"I know, I know — but uh — how about fixing up this place first?

"Hahh?"

"This place, dad, it's old. Why don't you change the lanterns or something?"

"The lanterns? Naah. What for? Waste my money. I'm selling this place."

A few weeks later, I mixed up one order too many at the restaurant, that's what my father said. He fired me —

in front of the customers and in front of the girl from China. She retreated to the kitchen door. I defended myself. "It's not me," I said. "It's the cook. He's the one getting it mixed up."

"Sure. You write English. He know only Chinese. What you expect?"

My father got angry when he saw that I dared challenge him. In front of other people, no less. He sent me home to my mother. My mother put me to work painting the house. She said, "We make everything nice. When you and Gary get it, no problem."

I painted the hall green, a cool, celadon green. The living room, the bathroom, I painted round the clock.

"White trim. Let's paint it white," I said.

"Go sleep," my mother told me.

"Do we paint Gary's room, too? I like his wall paper."

"Go sleep," my mother said. "Ah Loong, Ah Loong," she yelled at my father when he came home from the restaurant. "Look at her. Why you don't do something! Two nights already."

"Take way the paint," my father said.

"I did already. Yesterday. You think I'm dumb?"

"What happened?"

"She go buy more!"

When I finished painting my room, I went to Gary's and fell asleep. My parents were arguing. I didn't mind. It was familiar. When I woke up, they were still arguing. I lay in the dark and listened. The night had that stillness with no end; it would be hours until dawn.

My parents were speaking their native dialect. My mother tongue, my father tongue.

"Crazy girl," my father said.

"Your family," my mother told him.

"Mine?! Yours!"

"No," my mother was emphatic. "Yours. Your mother, exactly."

She paused at this point She always did. I knew what she would say next. "Can't you see?" I spoke the words for her. In the old dialect, "Can't you see?"

My mother tongue, my father tongue. There was so little I remembered of the language I knew in deepest childhood. What metaphors made me throw my tongue away? I could almost taste the blood still. Was it chink, was it jap? After my early battles here with other people's metaphors, I would not speak the sounds closest to me. I went out instead and reeled in miles of other people's utterances, I spun their lives round my tape machine, I listened to their stories, and always, I kept a vigilant ear to what lurked beneath the surface, below the line. Was it a spurious contamination? Modulation noise? Hiss? Or was it something external? Something amenable to direct action? A refrigerator not turned off? Turn it off. A phone still on? Pull it. A dog barking? Shoot it.

"You don't give her everything, she not like this." My father always has to have the last word.

"Give her everything!" my mother spit at him now. "What you mean? My daughter not supposed to have good clothes? New shoes? This not your stupid village."

"My village!"

"Yah. Yours."

My mother tongue, my father tongue. I had gone out and tuned my ear to other people, other lives.

"Aiiiiyaaa! "

I had looked for words elsewhere to replace the ones I threw away, yet here they were, still, the primal sounds, the first words I heard. Before English, before America, before speech.

"Maybe, maybe I better not come here. Maybe I better stay in China."

"And have her kill you because she's Red Guard?"

"Yah! Yah! That way we all crazy together. Why not!"

When I woke up, it was late. The smell of fresh paint was deep in my skull. I went to the kitchen for coffee. My mother was on the phone, my father at the table. When I walked in, my father said, "Eh, get her some coffee. Bing-ah —"

"Okay, okay," my mother spoke into the phone, "I go now."

"Was that Gary?" I said.

My mother looked guilty, "You want scramble egg?"

"She made biscuits." My father opened the stove.

"No, I want Gary to quit talking about me," I said.

"Gary not talking about you," my mother lied. She got out two eggs and cracked them. "Gary just make another hundred thousand."

"Hundred?" My father turned from the sink where he was setting down his cup.

"That all?" I said. "He didn't have anything new to add?"

"One phone call and three words, 'it's-a-go.' Hundred-thousand. I wonder, next phone call, what?" my mother whipped up the eggs. "You need a vacation, May. Gary say he got a new condo, Maui. Where's Maui?"

My mother poured the eggs into a skillet. She looked refreshed this morning. So did my father. They always looked like this after a good fight. Bright-eyed, bushy-tailed. I'd forgotten. Their arguments weren't arguments. Their arguments were morale builders. Cautionary dramas. Always, in the middle of the night, they scolded and frightened each other so they could awaken the next morning to work even harder. To strive anew. Like this, this morning.

The summer sun entered on their shoulders, the heat rose off the stove, they handed me their biscuits and eggs, and when they said, "Eat, eat, better eat it all up," I thought, where can I find, as Gary has, the language with which I can answer them.

I took my mother's car. She had finally learned to drive; she had a big old Oldsmobile. I drove her fat car that afternoon to the lake and swam straight for the sandbar. When I was little I had been too afraid to do this, to go out to the middle of the lake and paddle about until I found, in that flat nothing, a place to stand.

Now, I went straight out. I had walked the shores of the lake as a Girl Scout, mapped the trails going around. There was the summer camp to the north, the picnic tables under the pines to my left. I stroked to the sandbar. Other people were there already. Boys whacking water at each other. An old man paddling in circles. A canoe farther out.

It was so peaceful, so complete, I wondered what more could I find in this landscape, this placid day. A little figure in red walking the far shore? Some ancient Indian survived to this moment?

I stood on the sandbar, the lake up to my shoulders. I waited for a vision. All around, the shore continued dull and green. Sunbathers laid out like pale grubs on the dark rocks. The trees would not part.

I would have to look elsewhere. Beneath the surface, below the line, I dove and the lake met me, a cool rush, the first silence, the first sound. Perhaps here — I went for the sandbar that had frightened me as a child. Opened my eyes to the murk. Reached. Touched the rocks. Touched something else. An unseen arm. A leg. There was an explosion under me. Someone kicked. I kicked. And, jackknifing for the surface, the lake streaming past, I looked and saw pale limbs kicking into sunlight.

THERE WAS A WINDOW I became attached to; it showed a pair of tube socks and a pair of boxer shorts. The socks and shorts never left their window, never changed positions — socks to the left, shorts to the right. I never saw who owned them.

One day, a wrecking crew came and ripped out the street across the way. A whole block fell. The guts of what used to be spilled out over the neighborhood. Wire and steel, mauled as if Godzilla had laid waste to civilization. I became interested in what remained: six stories of toilets ascending to blue sky. Floor on floor of drainage left intact. I snapped pictures. Others came to snap pictures. In this time of amnesia, the socks and shorts disappeared. When I next remembered to look, a washcloth had taken their place. It hung by a corner, and soon vanished.

I noticed this at dusk one day, as the traffic was backing up. I looked across honking cars to that window above, and in a square of light, with the evening's discord rising all about, in the spot that had once displayed artifacts of modern life, a lone figure rose up and started an ancient dialogue: he harangued a wall. No one else appeared. Even so, the man continued on. And from where I stood in the honk of traffic, whatever he said, he said wordlessly.

## PRAISE FOR *BELOW THE LINE*

"*Below the Line* is a page-turner, a rich and satisfying collection of stories. The language is lean and elegant, the humor sly, the characters poignant, quirky, and all-too human, moving with jet-set ease from East to West, and back again. A realistic and fascinating depiction of the unglamorous, pennypinching world of independent movie-making provides a unique and often hilarious backdrop to most of these delightful stories. Sara Chin is a smart, welcome new voice in contemporary fiction."

—Jessica Hagedorn

"There is a poetic certainty in Sara Chin's movement of words that beckons the eye to linger then move along her melody of line and utter finesse of gesture; these are the best kind of stories: wry, with unexpected turns of a cinematic lens, they are culturally honest, written without fear."

— Lois-Ann Yamanaka

"In the visual business of video and film production, the audio technician, alone between earphones, *hears* the glitches in a world where everyone focuses on seeing. Sara Chin, with careful ear, takes the reader below the line where guttural utterances like *eh* and *uh* matter, where voice-over, dubbing, and background music fall away around a cake of tofu, where the sounds of immigrant life intrude on a muted screen filled with American signage and gesture. The crafted cadence of these stories and prose poems tweaks our ears and visual memories, reminding us of the reasons why we read, reminding us why the book is better than the movie."

— Karen Tei Yamashita

"Sara Chin writes with subtlety, wit, and feeling, taking us along on her 'hunt for love and history.' The narrator of this now poignant, now hilarious collection of skillfully written short stories admits being in love with 'the tangential, the ephemeral,' with what lurks beneath the surface and is thus 'below the line.' Chin finds in every small moment something as profound as the universe and as wide as the human heart. Which one of us cannot identify in some way with the lonely exile's tragicomic struggle for survival and meaning, like the immigrant father who, having made it through bombings and political upheavals in China, gets frantically lost circling the Washington, D.C. Beltway loop? These wonderful stories express a luminous intelligence and are told with humor and compassion."

— Elaine Kim